# Cash 'n' Carrots
# & other capers

PHIL SYPHE

Copyright © 2013 Phil Syphe

All rights reserved.

ISBN: 978-1484869444

# CONTENTS

Acknowledgments

Preface 1

1 Watch Your Back 3
2 Bad Language 33
3 Bats & Bellybuttons 36
4 Rising Aromas 50
5 The Dark Hander 58
6 A Proposal 74
7 Alternate Angles 80
8 Stunned 84
9 Where's Walter? 115
10 Ant Values 119
11 The Beauty of Railings 121
12 Splattered 129
13 Arrabella Wellfitt 132
14 Raspberries 142
15 Cash 'n' Carrots 147

# ACKNOWLEDGMENTS

Thanks to my former creative writing tutors for their guidance during my time at university: Martin Goodman, Bethan Jones, David Kennedy, Simon Kerr, Mary Nettleton, and Jim Younger. Special thanks to Ray French.

Thanks to the following for offering advice, giving feedback, or inspiring events in one story or another: Doug Armitage, Derek Bradley, Rachael Brocklebank, Danny Fisher, Denny Horozova, Jack Kelly, Charles Little, Joanna Morris, Ian Purkis, and my parents Pauline & Alan.

Although I am a copy-editor & proofreader, if I ever fail to spot a mistake it's in my own writing. Therefore, I'd like to say a big thank you to the following people for helping me with the proofreading:

Amber Carnegie (*The Beauty of Railings*), Jimi Holt (*Stunned*), and James Smart (*Rising Aromas*).

Thanks to Peter Kench for offering advice on several stories whilst at university and for proofreading *A Proposal*.

Special thanks to Zofia Wierzbinski for advising on several stories in this collection and for proofreading *Raspberries* and *Cash 'n' Carrots*.

Special thanks to Gill Curley for advising on several stories in this collection and for proofreading *Watch Your Back*, *Bats & Bellybuttons*, *The Dark Hander*, *Stunned*, *Arrabella Wellfitt*, and *Cash 'n' Carrots*.

# PREFACE

I wrote and revised *Bats & Bellybuttons*, *The Dark Hander*, and *Arrabella Wellfitt* during early 2013. I penned the other stories in this collection at various stages from 2009-2012 for creative writing exercises at the University of Hull. I spent time revising and extending them from April 2012. They were all finalised in April 2013.

# WATCH YOUR BACK

Tom assured Alec that if they could film Diana – the most desired woman in town – wearing a swimsuit they'd be able to sell copies of the footage to their friends. The two teenagers hid in wait for her to emerge from the ladies' changing rooms.

'Just think how much money we could make from this!' said Tom.

'Just think how much shit we'll be in if they catch us.'

'Women like her never notice guys like us. We're just boys to them.'

Diana, at twenty, was three years their senior. Coming from a rich family she was able to hire the pool for an hour every Sunday morning for herself and three female friends.

Tom endeavoured getting into the swimming baths two months ago, only to be turned away. He returned the subsequent week, plus the Sunday following that, keeping an eye on the security guard, observing that he took comfort breaks at more or less the same times. On the third week Tom chanced sneaking in and out of the building. When he managed to do this without being noticed he returned every week to spy on Diana. This time he'd persuaded his best friend to join him.

Tom asked Alec if he'd seen Diana's house.

'Course not!'

'It's massive! She even has a cabin in the woods.'

'How do you know all this?'

'Listen! Voices! Quick! Down here!'

They crouched out of sight as Diana and her friends exited the changing rooms. They chatted as they walked towards the pool, unaware of the camera filming them.

'Damn her groupies!' said Tom. 'They're swarming round her; can't get a clear shot.'

'Maybe that's a sign for us to go.'

'Hell! I couldn't even zoom in on her when they got into the pool. Those three seem more into her than we are.'

'Than *you* are, you mean. Let's go.'

'I've got another idea.'

They sneaked into the ladies' changing rooms.

Alec wiped his forehead. He was an athletic boy, lacking confidence, due to his spot-covered face. His eyes darted from the doorway to Tom, currently searching through Diana's belongings.

Tom wasn't as tall or as well built as Alec, but his complexion was clear and most girls of his age liked him, though Tom wasn't interested in teenage *girls*; he was attracted to *women*. And no woman proved more appealing than Diana.

'Damn it, Tom! Do you want to get arrested for theft as well as stalking?'

Tom pulled Diana's phone from her bag and switched it on.

'I just want to check her texts.'

'Why?'

'Interesting.' He winked at his red-cheeked friend. 'The recent messages in her inbox – all from her "clingy" friends – are about next Saturday. They're going to Whitehart Wood. More interesting still are her received and missed calls.'

'Can't you tell me about this later?' said Alec,

fidgeting in the doorway.

'What's interesting is that the calls are all from someone called Ryan.'

Tom switched the phone off and put it back in the bag.

'Fascinating. Can we get out of here now?'

Ten minutes later the teenagers were back in Tom's Skoda.

'What the hell was all that about?' said Alec, wiping sweat from his spotty brow. 'This was gonna be a bit of fun, according to you; making a bit of money from our fellow "no-hopers" by selling them the equivalent of "soft porn", as you put it.'

'And so we shall.'

Tom turned the key in the ignition.

'Why not use the footage of the other girls in their swimsuits?' said Alec, as they drove away.

'They're hot but nobody's gonna want to buy an amateur film of amateur beauties. They could watch that sort of thing for free on the internet. Diana, on the other hand, is a goddess. Why she's not a model or something other than a secretary, I don't know.'

'Probably because she's a well-paid secretary. Bet she earns a mint at that law firm.'

'That reminds me: I saw her talking to some guy outside her workplace last week. Maybe it was this "Ryan" character. He was a tall bloke. About six-foot six, I reckon.'

Tom parked outside Alec's house several minutes later.

'She's going to her woodland retreat on Saturday, leaving us five days to prepare.'

'Prepare for what?'

'I'll sort it. Just don't plan anything for next weekend.'

\*

Ryan worked as a lawyer for the same company who employed Diana. He stood as tall as Tom predicted, with a lean physique and a handsome face. His untiring perusal of Diana paid off after several weeks when she gave him her phone number. On the day Tom saw her talking to Ryan they were arranging to meet up outside of work, but the planned date did not proceed the way Ryan hoped.

Diana arrived at The Feisty Ferret Inn, accompanied by her friends Tamara, Tanya, and Tina. She waved at Ryan from the opposite end of the crowded pub.

He returned her wave, wearing a smile to mask the burning frustration he felt towards her for bringing three friends along. His rage cooled upon spying Diana weaving her way through the crowd towards him while the others headed to the bar. His anger vanished when she glided into the space where he stood in one corner of the room.

Diana had the type of smile that could soften the angriest of hearts. Such perfect teeth and luscious lips. Her beautiful eyes smiled too when she looked into Ryan's face. In him she saw a man of confidence who admired her, though not in a pathetic awestruck way.

Diana kissed Ryan's cheek and said, 'Sorry we're a bit late. Tina lost one of her contact lenses. It took us ages to find it.'

Diana stepped back after greeting her date. Three-inch heels meant she stood half a foot below Ryan. Shiny tights and a slinky dress made the gorgeous brunette more noticeable than usual.

Ryan asked what she'd like to drink.

'Tamara's getting me a gin and tonic, thanks.'

'Why is *she* buying you one?'

'It's her round. What's that?' Diana pointed at the half-pint glass in Ryan's hand. 'Vodka and orange?'

'No, just orange. Thought you might want driving home later.'

'My brother's giving me a lift.'

Ryan opened his mouth to speak, but was rendered

mute for a few minutes, as Diana's friends swarmed round her. Why were they even there? This was a date for two, not five.

Ryan pointed at a free table at the other end of the pub. Diana could just see it through a gap between punters. The quintet headed that way. Diana stopped as they drew nearer.

'There's only enough room for four. We'll have to – ah! Over there!'

She pointed at a long seat against the wall.

They walked over and sat, from left to right, Tamara, Tanya, Tina, Diana, Ryan.

During the next two hours Ryan never once had his date to himself. The women always went to the toilet in pairs, except if Diana needed to go, then all four of them paid a visit. This didn't mean Ryan was being ignored though. Diana enjoyed chatting to him, but her ignorance regarding their 'date' was causing a tightening in Ryan's stomach, coupled with a raging thunderstorm in his mind. If he'd been drinking he wouldn't have accepted this scenario without causing a fuss. Even so, his patience frayed as time progressed. When, after another hour elapsed, the women started discussing their preferred colour schemes for their perfect 'dream house', Ryan asked Diana for a word in private.

The pair returned to the corner where they first met that evening.

'I thought it'd be just the two of us tonight. All this girl-talk's getting on my nerves. I'm gonna book a taxi so I can drink. A beer would go down well right now.'

Diana struggled to perceive him word for word, owing to the pub's music pumping through a speaker above their heads. She was further distracted by her brother's appearance in the doorway.

She shouted to make herself heard: 'Time for me to go, but –'

'What!' Ryan bellowed into her ear. 'It's only quarter

past ten!'

She wiped the spittle from her face.

'It's the only time my brother can take me home.'

'I'll drive you! We can stay out as long as we want.'

'Thanks, but I arranged the lift especially. Paul won't be happy if I say I've decided to stay out longer.' Ryan intended to declare how much he cared for Paul's happiness until Diana added: 'I could see you tomorrow if you want? I'm going to my cabin in Whitehart Wood for the afternoon and staying overnight. Would you like to come down for a bit?'

Ryan opened his mouth to reply when Diana's twin brother Paul joined them. Just as Diana was by far the most beautiful woman in town, and for miles around, Paul was the most handsome man. He wasn't as tall as Ryan, though he boasted a more muscular physique.

The men exchanged greetings by nodding. Their eyes met for an instant, each casting a look of suspicion on the other.

Diana asked Paul to wait outside. She'd join him in a minute. He assented.

Meanwhile, Ryan felt his impatience was going to cause his head to explode. Once Paul moved away, he returned to the subject of Whitehart Wood. He knew where it was, though had never been there. When Diana announced she'd be going to the cabin at two o'clock tomorrow afternoon, Ryan promised to arrive at two thirty.

He placed his hands on Diana's trim waist, about to pull her towards him for a kiss on the lips, but she pulled away when her friends came over. She gave him a rub on his arm and wished him goodnight.

Ryan drove home via the off-licence, treating himself to four pint-sized cans of lager. He consumed the first one in about five minutes. The night had been a disaster yet all was not lost. He figured Diana had been testing him. He'd done well not to lose his temper. Staying sober proved a worthwhile endeavour after all. Tomorrow would be his day. An afternoon in the woods with the most beautiful woman he'd ever seen, followed by an undisturbed night of passion in a little cabin. Diana would be his greatest conquest. Obviously she felt the same about him and wanted them to be together somewhere isolated.


Saturday morning. Tamara, Tanya, and Tina stood with Diana, about to enter her white Jaguar, when a beeping horn turned their heads. A Toyota screeched around the corner, halting near the kerb.

Paul stepped out and swaggered towards his sister.

Diana said, 'You three get in the car. This won't take long.'

Paul said, 'Where're you going?'

'Where do you think?'

Diana glanced down at her white outfit and trainers.

'Isn't that skirt too tight for playing tennis? Must you show so much cleavage? Do –'

'Do you have to question me every time I go out?'

Paul folded his muscular arms while his sister ponytailed her dark-brown tresses.

'Where are your rackets?'

'In the boot. Want to check?'

'I just hope you're not meeting that guy from last night. I didn't like him.'

'You don't like anybody! If that's all, I'm going.'


Ryan slowed his Ferrari down after turning onto the narrow track leading to Whitehart Wood. He smiled when the cabin came into view. The building was situated in a large clearing. He parked near a row of trees. Unable to relax at home, he'd set off early, thus arriving three-quarters of an hour before Diana's appointed time.

Ryan traipsed over to the nearest line of trees at the

far side of the cabin, sauntering here for several minutes before taking a circuit around the building. He paused near the three steps leading up to the walkway, gazing across at his car. After plodding up the steps Ryan slid on his shades and sat on the bench under the living room window with the sun shining over him. He'd overdressed. Shorts would've been more appropriate, but he wanted to look smart in shoes, trousers, and a shirt, thinking this would make a good impression on Diana. After the tiresome build up of the evening before, surely it should only be a matter of time until clothes would no longer be of importance anyway.

From two o'clock Ryan frequently checked his watch. Forty-five minutes later he was pacing up and down, cursing Diana for being late. Okay, he'd told her he'd arrive at two thirty, but she should have been there at two.

Three o'clock came round. Ryan ran his fingers through his gelled hair and wiped the beads of sweat from his brow. Where was she? Five past three. Enough!

Ryan stormed towards his Ferrari, cursing Diana under his breath – but wait! Were his ears playing tricks on him or could he hear a vehicle in the distance? Yes, a car was approaching. Back to the cabin. He sat down, pretending to be talking to someone on his phone, just as the Jaguar materialised.

'I'm not even giving her a sideways glance until she's nearly on me,' said Ryan to the non-existent person on the other end of his mobile.

Yet he looked over sooner than intended when four car doors opened and closed.

'In the name of shite they'd better just be dropping her off!'

The four women in white strolled over, each carrying a little rucksack. Tanya and Tamara also held a larger bag between them containing food and drink.

'Sorry we're late,' said Diana, making her way up the walkway steps. 'Have you been waiting long?'

'Not really. I was late myself. Guess you've been playing tennis?'

'No, we dressed like this for my brother's benefit. He'd gate-crash us if he knew we were here.' Diana unlocked the cabin door. 'We're going to get some food and drink from the kitchen to go with what we've brought and head off to my favourite spot in the woods.'

Ryan followed her inside. The others were chirping behind him.

'Is it far?' Ryan hoped he didn't sound as aggravated as he felt. 'My shoes aren't designed for forest trekking.'

They entered the little kitchen.

'No, it's not – just put that food on the table, thanks, Tamara – no, Ryan, it's not far. We'll walk slow –'

'Excuse me,' said Tanya. 'Does this other bottle of wine want putting in the fridge or the cupboard?'

'Cupboard, please. We'll take the other one with us.'

Two minutes' worth of women buzzing around him in the small kitchen pushed Ryan's patience to the limit, especially when every time he tried to engage Diana into a conversation someone interrupted.

'I'll wait outside,' he said, with clenched fists and a racing heart.

'Oh, okay. We won't be long.'

'You'd better not, for shite's sake,' said Ryan under his breath, heading down the short corridor from kitchen to front door.

They weren't long, though it was a wait Ryan could've done without. Being asked to carry a large blanket added insult to his injury.

They commenced a slow walk to accommodate for Ryan's inappropriate footwear. Within ten minutes they reached a large oval clearing in the woods. Diana spread the blanket on the ground. Here she and the other women seated themselves next to a large log where Ryan sat.

He was content eating the sausage rolls and sandwiches on offer, along with drinking more than his share from their bottle of red wine, though he was less impressed with listening to the women's constant chatter. Diana kept trying to involve him in their conversations, but his temper had risen too high for him to want to join in. He wished Tamara, Tanya, and Tina would get lost and let him take Diana to bed.

Over half an hour elapsed, leaving Ryan with no more wine to distract himself.

'Have you any more of this?'

He held the empty bottle upside down.

'That didn't last long,' said Diana, kneeling upright. 'I've only had one glass. Luckily we brought two bottles.' She rose. 'I'll go fetch it.'

'Shall we all go?' said Tamara.

'No!' said Ryan, shooting to his feet. 'Diana can get the wine without assistance! I'll join her for the walk. I'm not used to sitting around on a log all day listening to birds chirp and chatter.'

Diana and Ryan set off for the cabin.

'Why are those women here?' His pent-up irritation now showed in his tone of voice and facial expression. 'Can't you get rid of them? I thought today was your way of making up for last night's disaster.'

'Disaster? I thought we had a pleasant evening until my brother had to take me home.'

'Oh yeah, he was the icing on the cake.'

Diana was stuck for words. She thought Ryan liked her company. They walked on in silence until the cabin was in sight.

'I'm sorry if my friends being here bothers you –'

'Course it bothers me! Last night turned into a joke because of them and today's been a bloody nightmare! Let's get this wine taken back – for us *two* to drink – and then you can tell those three dizzy blonde bitches to shit off!'

'How *dare* you talk to me like that!' Diana's soft brown eyes changed to blazing fires. 'And my friends are *not* "dizzy blonde bitches", thank you very much!'

They made their way up the three steps to the cabin. Ryan tried to calm himself down as Diana took out her keys. If his temper blew up he'd lose any chance of getting intimate with the most beautiful of women. He remained silent as they entered the building; his eyes glued to Diana's bottom and bare thighs as he followed her down the corridor.

Moments later the pair faced each other in the kitchen.

'I didn't mean to sound off like that.' Ryan fought to keep his anger in check. 'I just expected last night to be a proper date. When it wasn't I presumed today would be for sure. I've nothing against your friends, only how can we spend time alone if they're here?'

'Well we're alone now and all we've done is argue.'

'Okay. No more arguing, though can't we have some time away from the others?'

The fire left Diana's eyes and they softened again. She smiled, thinking she was right about Ryan after all. He was a sweet guy really; just feeling neglected through her not giving him enough attention. She took out the bottle of red wine from the cupboard and handed Ryan the bottle.

'Will you carry this for me? I'll have a word with the girls when we get back. Maybe the two of us could wander down one of the woodland tracks together. I know a few routes you might like.'

'Okay.' This sounded like a step in the right direction. 'Any chance of me opening this now? I could do with another drink.'

'If you like.' Diana smiled, taking a bottle opener from a drawer and a glass from a cupboard. 'Just don't have too much in case you go over the driving limit.'

'Driving? I took it for granted I'd be staying here tonight.'

He slammed the glass on the kitchen worktop and popped open the bottle.

'I didn't invite you here for a dirty weekend.'

'What the hell have you invited me here for, huh?'

Ryan filled the half-pint glass as Diana wandered past him, heading for the living room next door. He guzzled the entire glass of wine and followed with bottle in hand.

The living room, although small, was the largest area in the building. The walls were painted blue, matching the carpet. A navy two-seated couch stood against the longest wall on the left. Two matching armchairs were placed at opposite ends of the room.

When Ryan entered he found Diana stood looking at the floor. Her stern gaze fell on him as he drew near. She indicated for him to take a seat. He chose the chair with its back to the window.

'This beats numbing my arse on a fallen tree,' he said, plonking down on the soft cushion.

Diana sat facing him with folded arms and crossed legs. She found his tone and choice of words offensive. She shook her head when he took a drink from the bottle.

'Can't you use the glass I just gave you?'

'I like to get straight to the point. I don't like wasting time or being taken for a ride. Why the hell did you invite me out last night and here today if you don't fancy me?'

'I do – or did – fancy you. I thought you were genuinely interested in me as a person, not just as a bed partner.'

'How naïve are you? You don't give a bloke all these bloody come-ons for nothing unless you're a cock-tease.'

Ryan muttered something inaudible before taking another guzzle of wine.

'I'm not a tease, it's just … Listen, I haven't told many people this, but maybe if I explain you'll understand why I'm cautious.'

'Cautious! Contraceptives are the only cautions you need to worry about, for shite's sake! What the hell do you mean by "cautious"?'

'I was about to explain before you cut me off. If you

don't stop speaking to me like that I won't tell you a damn thing.'

Diana stared daggers at Ryan, showing him she wouldn't continue without an apology. He guessed a night of passion was out of the question now, yet an explanation of why she'd led him on might at least satisfy his mind.

'Okay. Sorry. What were you going to say?'

Diana took a deep breath before commencing her story.

'Aged fifteen, a boy at school came on to me when I was alone one dinner break. We had two sets of cloakrooms; one big, one small. The smallest was in the quietest area of the building, meaning you were least likely to encounter anybody. On this particular day I'd left my science book in a class near these cloakrooms. As I walked by, a sixteen-year-old boy called Gary appeared, blocking my path, saying he'd only let me pass if I promised to go out with him. When I refused his request, he refused mine to get by. I threatened to shout for one of the teachers. Gary stepped aside, but followed me as I walked away.

'As I was about to pass the boys' toilets Gary grabbed me from behind. An arm went around my waist, a hand smothered my mouth. He dragged me backwards into the toilets, muttering what he was going to do to me. By pure luck my brother was there, drying his hands. Paul dragged Gary off me. Gary never bothered me again. In fact he didn't come back to school any more.

'Being grabbed like that unnerved me for a long time. I also toughened up because of it. Paul, on the other hand, became paranoid about me getting raped every time I left our house. He made me swear not to get intimate with anybody and avoid being alone with men before my twenty-first birthday. Ever since we were children we've always kept our word if we swear to be true to something. So far I've had no regrets about making my promise.'

Diana released a deep sigh after relating these past events.

Meanwhile, Ryan had listened without interrupting, taking regular gulps of wine. Now he spoke in a mocking tone.

'You mean to say you've never slept with anybody? And you're twenty? Come on!'

Diana sighed, looking away. Her right foot flicked the air.

'When are you twenty-one?'

'In ten weeks,' said Diana, renewing eye contact.

'So you were gonna dick me around for ten weeks? Then what? Make me wait another three months in case your brother gets upset?'

'You would never have been invited here if I'd known you were like this! I liked you because you seemed charming and confident, but you're just an arrogant pig!'

'And you are a cock-teasing bitch! Expecting me to believe that story! What shite!'

'You'd better leave.'

Diana glared at him with volcanic eyes.

Ryan was about to speak when a barking dog distracted him.


Long before Ryan and Diana met at the cabin, Alec waited with a tight stomach for Tom to knock on his door.

'Why do I let him talk me into these things?' he said to his reflection in the bathroom mirror as he applied Acnehilate Cream to his legion of spots.

Why indeed? Alec often asked himself this question. The only answer he could ever produce was that it beat staying home alone. He didn't have many friends. Those he did have all had girlfriends. Alec believed other people found him boring. Perhaps Tom did too, though he always had time for him. Alec had stayed on at school, whereas Tom got himself a job working in a DVD rental store, hence why he could afford a car – even if it was a clapped-out Skoda.

All this business of following Diana, filming her, taking photos of her to sell, was getting out of control. Alec thought she was the most stunning woman in town just like everybody else did, but what he and Tom were doing was beginning to feel wrong. Okay, it *was* wrong. At first it struck him as innocent fun. Now he felt Tom was pushing his luck. Just because they didn't intend Diana any harm it didn't mean she wouldn't care if she caught them following her. He did not at all believe in Tom's theory that she'd be flattered if she found out about their 'devotion' to her.

'She's hardly going to give us a medal for best stalkers,' was Alec's view.

Tom arrived at one o'clock. The pair set off on their expedition wearing shorts and T-shirts, each carrying a rucksack on their back. Tom brought his Golden Labrador puppy along. Having walked for over an hour, they paused halfway down the roadside, adjacent to the wood.

'Let's have a snack,' said Tom, removing his rucksack. 'See that gap in the trees?'

'That's not much of a gap, but yeah, I see it.'

'That's our way in.'

Tom sat beside his tail-wagging puppy.

'Why don't we go down the lane that leads to the main track?' said Alec, also sitting.

'In case Diana thinks we're following her.'

'We *are* following her.'

'Yes, but we don't want her to know that, do we?'

'I bloody well don't!'

After resting on the grass bank, basking in the sunshine for a few minutes, Tom rose, saying, 'Come on! I've been this way a few times.' He slung his rucksack on his back and set off. 'I know these woods well.'

Alec felt butterflies gather in his stomach as he approached the first line of trees.

They delved into the woodland. Although the route they took had no track marked out, Tom found no difficulty navigating between trees, eventually bringing them to the clearing not far from the cabin where Ryan and the women arrived for their picnic several minutes earlier.

'Yes!' said Tom. 'I thought they'd come here again.'

'Again? You mean you've seen them here before?'

'Yeah, about half a dozen times.'

'So you've –'

'Give Amber some of her treats. We don't want her barking now.'

Tom slid off his rucksack, unzipped it, and took out a bag of broken biscuits. He handed them to Alec. He crawled nearer to the clearing, keeping himself hidden behind the foot of a tree.

'That tall guy's holding a bottle upside down.' Tom switched on the camera. 'Shit! Dumb, Dumber, and Dumbest are in the way – ah! Diana's kneeling up! Whoa! She's wear –'

'Keep your voice down!'

'They won't hear me from this distance! Diana's wearing a sexy tennis outfit! I know lots of lads who've got a thing for girls in tennis whites.'

'Me too. I'm looking at one of them.'

Tom crawled back a few minutes later and grabbed his rucksack.

'She's walking off with Stretch. Let's follow them.'

The teens pursued them unobserved through the trees, stopping ten minutes later at the edge of the wood bordering the open space around the cabin, just as Diana and Ryan were about to head indoors.

'She could be ages,' said Alec.

'Hopefully – I've hidden some webcams inside.'

'What!'

'I followed Diana to the swimming baths three weeks before you joined me and used plasticine to copy her keys. I came here yesterday evening to set the cameras up.'

'You broke into her property?'

'No, I used the key.'

'Oh, well that's okay then! You didn't put a camera in the bathroom, did you?'

'Everywhere but there.'

'Glad you've got *some* respect for her privacy.'

'No, it's not that. There was nowhere to hide a camera in the bathroom.'

'Bloody hell, Tom! How did you find out about this place, anyway?'

'Diana came to the DVD store about two months ago. I heard her catting with the blonde airheads about her parents buying the cabin in Whitehart Wood. Apparently they're letting her use it for the summer while they travel across Europe. That family must be bloody loaded. Now you can understand why Diana can afford to use that swimming pool privately on Sundays. Man, if only there was a way we could share that pool with them!'

Suddenly a rabbit hopped into Amber's view. Tom didn't have a good grasp of her lead. He failed to stop the barking dog from charging after the rabbit. The boys chased after the puppy, shouting at her to come back. The rabbit zoomed past the cabin towards the cars and disappeared from view. Amber gave up the hunt. She returned to the boys, tail wagging, lead in mouth.

'Bloody dog!' said Tom, grabbing the lead and patting her head – he could hardly stay angry when those fun-filled eyes stared up at him.

The chase brought them in front of the cabin. Alec noticed the net curtains twitch.

'Shitting hell! We've been seen!'

'Don't panic. If they ask questions, we're walking Amber.' Tom had brought her as a cover. 'If neither the goddess nor the ogre comes outside in the next few minutes we'll go.'

'Let's go now!'

'No, the camera's on. I might be able to sneak a decent close-up of her.'

'Or you might cause a punch up with that tall guy, especially if he sees that camera.'

'Don't forget, it's switched on because we're filming Amber having fun.'

Ryan put the wine on the floor and peered through the living room window when the dog barked outside. He watched Tom, Alec, and Amber for a few moments, making sure they didn't go near his car. Once they moved off in the opposite direction he turned to find Diana missing. The door had been left open all along, hence why he didn't hear her move whilst gazing outside. He snatched the wine bottle from the floor and took another drink. Just as he was about to look for Diana, she returned, holding up her phone.

'Just fetched my mobile from the kitchen.'

'Who are those two boys outside with the dog?'

'No idea.' She sat down again. 'People walk by here sometimes. It's not a private wood, but this is my private property, and I want you off it.'

Ryan stood motionless, ogling Diana's toned figure and perfect face, before taking another mouthful of wine. He was about to speak when Diana's phone bleeped a text alert.

'Is that one of the tiresome trio wondering how you could leave them for more than ten minutes?'

'It's my brother. I sent him a text whilst in the kitchen, asking him to come here in case you refuse to leave. The way Paul drives he'll only be twenty minutes, maybe sooner. You'd better go now.'

'I'm not scared of him.'

He sat down.

For two minutes the only sound was the occasional glug when Ryan took a drink.

'Listen,' he said, breaking the silence, 'I've got a lot of influence at work. A word in the right ear could improve your employment situation. Tell your brother to stay away and let's head to the bedroom.'

'Right!' Diana slid one leg off the other and slapped her knees. 'I'll show you out.'

She rose. Ryan remained seated, assuring her he could just as easily get her sacked.

'Well you'll never get me *in* the sack!'

She stood in the open doorway. Fury burned in her eyes.

'All right, I'll go, but I need a piss first.'

Diana strolled outside onto the walkway while Ryan visited the bathroom. She saw Alec, Tom, and Amber heading towards the first line of trees leading into the woods. Hearing the toilet flush, she faced the cabin.

Ryan stepped outside, rolling his shirt sleeves up above the elbow, greeting her with a burp.

'You're too drunk to drive. I suggest you walk to the top road, catch a bus, and collect your car tomorrow.'

'I'm not leaving my car here, for shite's sake!'

'You'll have to. You're inebriated.'

'I'll sleep on the back seat.'

'We intend staying here till tomorrow. I don't want you barging in on us during the middle of the night. Please leave.'

She turned to close the cabin door.

'I am leaving, but you're coming with me.'

'No,' she said, locking the door, 'I'm heading back –'

'That wasn't a question.'

Diana – back turned – was slipping her key into a small inner-pocket inside the waistline of her skirt when he grabbed her.

Ryan – encircling Diana's waist with one long arm, and covering her entire lower face with a huge palm – said, 'I would've thought a retreat like this would be the perfect getaway for two, yet it seems like a place for social gatherings.' He edged backwards towards the steps. 'Let's go somewhere private before your brother, or more dog walkers, or the three dozy cows, or shite-knows-who turns up!'

Diana may have been at a disadvantage, but she was a tall, athletic, *sober* woman. Ryan's head swam with alcohol, lust, and rage. When he lifted his foot to step down – backwards – Diana, instead of trying to pull forwards and away from him, forced herself *into* him. He slipped, tumbling down the steps, making a decent cushion for Diana who rolled off him once they'd landed. She emitted a scream for help as she broke free. Ryan made it to his hands and knees just as Diana rose and made her first step towards her car. Rather than trying to rise, Ryan made a lunge from his floored position, outstretching his long arms. Diana screamed again when four tentacle-like fingers and a thumb enveloped her slender ankle. His tight grasp, backed up by his bodyweight, brought her face-down to the ground, winding and dazing her with the impact.

Ryan still gripped Diana as he rose. He seized her other ankle with his opposite hand and twisted her over, inflicting further pain when she cracked her head on a large stone. He raised her legs off the floor and shuffled backwards towards his car.

Diana cushioned the back of her head with both hands as Ryan dragged her across the bumpy surface.

'Let go of me!' she kept yelling.

He halted at the rear of his Ferrari, releasing one ankle to pop open the car boot.

Diana screamed louder than ever as Ryan locked one arm round her thighs while another snaked under her back. She landed several punches against his jaw, plus a few scratches to his cheek, yet nothing slowed him down. She was also out of time.

'You bastard!' she said, banging her head, crashing inside the car boot.

Ryan forced Diana's kicking legs in after her before shutting the boot.

'Now let's find a layby or something where we can –

what the …'


The teens had just delved amongst the trees when Diana's first scream caught their attention. Amber started barking and tail-wagging while they exchanged open-mouthed glances before hurrying to the nearest tree bordering the open area around the cabin.

'Whoa!' said Tom, spying Diana and Ryan on the floor. 'Quick! Take Amber's lead! Let's film them fooling around.'

'Shit! They're not messing around! She's trying to get away from – shit!'

Alec didn't feel Amber's lead straining against his hand when Ryan began hauling Diana across the ground.

'Shit, Tom! What we gonna – stop bloody filming, for f –'

'Calm down! Just – hey!'

Alec swatted at the camera, almost knocking it from Tom's hand.

'We need to do something!'

Alec stood with one foot near the tree, the other in the open space. Amber's lead dug into his hand as she strained to get near the action.

Tom said, 'Best we can do is not get involved. If – Amber!'

The Labrador shuttled off towards the two parked vehicles as Ryan locked Diana in his car boot.

Ryan hadn't noticed the puppy's constant barking whilst preoccupied with Diana, but as he turned away from his Ferrari the first thing he saw was the excited dog charging towards him. His eyes darted in every direction. Where were the boys? Had they seen him?

'Gooarn, dog! Gooarn!'

Ryan stomped the floor as Amber approached. She came to an abrupt halt, not understanding the tall man's strange reaction to her. She stood still, tail wagging, tongue hanging out between barks, curious about the shouts and banging noises coming from inside the car boot.

Ryan grabbed a small stone and threw it at Amber.

'Gooarn! Get!'

The puppy sped off but returned as Ryan walked an uneven line towards his car door. Amber didn't follow him. The unexplained activity emanating from the boot proved more interesting. Plus the tall man had thrown a stone at her.

'Shite, shite, shite!' was Ryan's response, sitting in the driving seat, seeing the reflection of Tom and Alec in his mirror. 'How much did those little shitehawks see?'

Alec had grabbed the biggest fallen branch he could find and marched towards the Ferrari. Tom hovered several paces behind, trying to convince him this wasn't their business.

Ryan stepped out of the car. The boys would hear Diana now, whether they saw what happened earlier or not. Either a pay-off or a threat of GBH would resolve the situation. He stood before the car boot.

'You've got to let her go,' said Alec, raising the heavy branch in shaky hands.

'How about a grand each for your silence? Don't worry, I'm not gonna kill her.'

'That's a lot of money,' said Tom to his friend.

Ryan smiled, realising he was winning them over.

Alec's temples throbbed. His palms, back, and forehead beaded with sweat. His ears were filled with a mixture of Diana's shouts and hammering, the sound escaping Amber's mouth, and the pounding of his own heart. Alec believed Ryan didn't intend to kill Diana, however, an athletic woman like her would put up a fight, which may lead to a manslaughter case. Even if that didn't happen it seemed obvious that Ryan had rape on his mind. Dragging a woman through the dirt by her ankles and locking her in a car boot was hardly a romantic gesture or the build up to a loving marriage proposal.

Ryan's smile vanished when the spotty youth darted forward wielding the branch. Ryan grasped the other end as it swung at him, yanking it from Alec's hands. Alec cried out as three or four strips of skin tore from his palms. Ryan threw the weapon at him. Alec ducked out of the way.

Amber stopped barking and bit the narrowest end of the branch. She started running around in circles with it while the fight continued.

They edged away from the car. Ryan had the height and weight advantage. Alec had the convenience of wearing more suitable clothes for a brawl plus he wasn't drunk.

Diana continued to scream and hammer from inside the boot. Amber ran alongside Tom, still holding the branch, while her master jogged over to the Ferrari. He switched his camera on, holding it in his left hand, as he pressed open the boot with his right.

'Argh!'

He jumped backwards after receiving a punch in his eye. Diana had lashed out as the boot opened.

'Sorry, sorry, sorry!' she said, climbing out of the car. 'I thought you were that pig – oh!' She pressed her hands to her cheeks, becoming aware of the fight nearby. 'Is that your friend?' Tom nodded. 'We'll help as soon as – ah!' She turned back to the boot, claiming the object that had been digging into her posterior during her captivity. 'I'll threaten Ryan with this!' She held up a huge spanner. 'There's nothing else in – I know! Grab that branch from the dog. Come on!'

Tom never thought he would not want to follow Diana, but in watching Alec struggle against the giant Ryan, he tugged the branch from Amber with reluctance.

The fighters had veered away from the cars. Alec had landed most of his blows against his opponent's body. He didn't have the reach to land many on Ryan's face. For the taller man this was no problem. Had Alec been less athletic and Ryan more sober he would've fallen long before now. Those temples that had pulsed with anxiety now throbbed with pain.

Crash! Alec hit the deck. Several hard kicks to the stomach ensured he stayed down. Ryan faced Diana and Tom just as a Toyota burst onto the scene. Everyone glanced towards Paul when he bolted from the car like an enraged bull. Amber pranced towards him as he stormed over. The puppy froze for a moment, wondering why this newcomer ignored her, though she soon put this rejection behind her and hurtled back towards her master.

Tom breathed a sigh of relief, aware that this was Diana's brother. Surely the out-of-breath drunk wouldn't last long against the muscular Paul.

'You okay, Diana?' said her brother, his eyes flicking between Tom beside her, Ryan a few paces away, and Alec moaning on the ground.

'That bastard was going to rape me! If it wasn't for these two –'

Paul didn't need to hear another word. He marched over to Ryan, raging a barrage of punches to his body. Unlike Alec, he could land blows against Ryan's face, however, he was so infuriated that Ryan, who'd released his pent-up aggression on Alec, was more in control despite his intake of alcohol.

Ryan did not retaliate at first. He concentrated on defence. Even so, with the wine affecting his reactions, Paul managed to deliver many damaging punches. Ryan backed towards his car. Escape from the scene was paramount.

Tom knelt beside his injured friend, Diana stood clutching the big spanner, while Amber barked, jumped, ran, and pranced around them.

As Ryan's back touched the side of his car, Paul caught him with a swift jab to the chin, unbalancing him. Ryan's long arms grappled around Paul, turning the punch-up into a wrestle. Paul slammed him against the Ferrari.

Ryan brought his knee up into Paul's groin and got a hand on his throat. He forced himself from the car, spun round, and slammed Paul against the vehicle, cracking his head against the hard surface. His grip slackened, allowing Ryan to smash his head a second time with more force. Paul crumpled to the floor, beaten. Ryan, gasping for breath, stepped backwards from the car, staring down at Paul, relieved it was over ... but he'd forgotten about Diana.

With both hands grasping the large spanner, she struck his shoulder from behind. He yelled, turning round. Diana crouched down and swung the spanner against his knee. He staggered forward, screaming, clutching his knee. She aimed for Ryan's shoulder again, but he jutted forwards, meeting her thunderous attack with his left temple. She dropped the blood-stained tool on the floor next to the limp figure.

Tamara, Tanya, and Tina had been making their way back from the woodland. They were aghast at what they saw, appearing just after Paul had been beaten. Diana hadn't heard them shouting. Only when the women hovered around her did the realisation of her actions take hold. Her friends tried hugging her all at once. She broke away from them, remembering her brother. She knelt beside him whilst the others fluttered in the background like moths near a light. Paul met her gaze, managing to smile for a second. Diana helped him sit upright.

'I feel like I've been run over by a herd of buffalo.' He massaged his head. 'What happened to that bastard? Did you and that boy overpower him or has he run off?'

She couldn't speak, but Tanya burst in with: 'Diana killed Ryan with a spanner!'

Alec – his nose bleeding – and Tom slouched towards them. For once Tom wasn't staring at Diana's body. His eyes were drawn to *the* body.

After Tamara phoned the emergency services she, Tanya

and Tina made their statements to the police. Diana, Paul, and Alec were taken to the local hospital. None of their injuries were serious, but the men were kept in overnight.

After Tom had been questioned by the police he hung around the cabin until he'd managed to reclaim all his hidden cameras.

In the evening he drove to the hospital where he found Alec in a four-bedded room.

'That was a close!' he said, sitting at his friend's bedside.

Alec nodded. He felt like one big ache. He furrowed his battered brow, noticing Tom's black eye.

'I don't remember you getting involved with the fighting. Did that shithead blacken your eye when I first went down?'

'Nah, Diana did it by accident when I let her out of the boot.'

'Sounds like some kind of justice to me.'

'It was anything *but* justice! I had the camera poised, hoping for a great up-skirt shot when she got out of the boot, only for her to bugger up all chances of that by whacking me.'

'How thoughtless of her. I guess you're gonna stop this stalking business after today?'

'Eh? Why should we stop now? If it wasn't for us she could've been raped or killed.'

'Hell, Tom! You –'

'Knock! Knock!'

Diana entered the room, wearing a heart-melting smile.

Tom shot to his feet, tipping his chair over.

'I hope you don't mind me paying you a visit?'

The lads shook their heads in silence.

Diana addressed Alec as she approached the bed.

'My brother keeps dozing off. He told me to get a taxi home. I felt I had to see you before going.' Turning to Tom: 'I'm glad you're here too – ooh, that eye!' She pressed her hands to her cheeks. 'Can you forgive me?'

Tom nodded and said 'Yeah' about ten times.

'Do you mind if I sit down for five minutes?'

This was like asking a starving lion if it fancied snacking on a wildebeest.

'Stay as long as you like,' said Tom, not believing his luck.

Diana smiled, sitting beside him.

Tom was in his element; sat so close to his 'Goddess'. He only wished he'd brought his camera. He could've pulled his mobile from his pocket and tried sneaking a couple of photos, though she'd surely notice at such close quarters. Plus she'd already killed one man today for showing too much interest in her.

Facing Tom, Diana said, 'Things would've been much worse if you two hadn't gone walking today. What a stroke of good fortune you were filming your cute little puppy and forgot to switch the camera off when Ryan – the bastard! – was dragging me to his car!'

'Such a lucky coincidence,' said Alec, colouring up.

'That's so true!' Diana patted her chest. 'Not only did you guys stop Ryan – the arrogant bastard! – from *trying* to rape me – I think he would've been too drunk to do anything serious, though he still could've sexually assaulted me – but not only that, if you hadn't decided to film that lovely Labrador today you wouldn't have caught so much on film and' – she touched Tom's forearm when she spoke – 'luckily you hadn't put your camera down when I whacked Ryan – the bloody arrogant bastard! – proving I was defending myself. Thank you both so much!' She hugged Tom, unaware of the sensations she caused to rush through his mind and body. 'I won't do that to you, Alec.' She stood, leaning over him. 'I know you're in some pain. A kiss won't hurt though, will it?' She gave him a peck on the lips, turning Tom rather green. 'I'll tell you both something,' she continued, sitting back down, brightening Tom up again, 'I'm not letting what happened today get to me. I can tell it's affected you, Alec. Don't let it bring you down. No way is that detestable bloody arrogant bastard going to haunt me! I'm not glad he's dead, and I do wish I hadn't killed him, but what happened was through his own actions. I'm not at fault. Feeling guilty is not an option. Anyway,' she rose, 'I've got to go.' She took out her mobile. 'Can I take your numbers?'

Tom said yes for them both. Diana texted them her number. Tom already knew it, of course.

'Sometimes my parents have parties at home,' she said, hovering near the end of the bed, 'so expect a text invite whenever there's a social gathering. Speaking of which, my twenty-first's coming up. Text me your addresses and I'll send you each an official invite. Do you fancy it?'

'We do fancy it,' said Tom, wide-eyed, grinning from ear to ear.

'Also, I'd like some of the evening on film. Would you mind doing the honours? I'll pay you for it, obviously.'

Tom returned Diana's radiant smile with the look of a man who had just won a fortune and been asked out on a date by his dream woman.

'I'll film more than enough footage. If you want, I could bring Amber and photograph you both together.'

'Thanks. Aww, I'd love to have my picture taken with that adorable dog! You two will have to bring her down to the cabin for an afternoon when Alec's feeling better. After what's happened it's going to feel a bit eerie in those woods. Give it a couple of weeks and we'll put this ghost to rest and visit the cabin.' Diana strolled towards the open doorway. 'Even though I'm not letting what's happened affect my life, it'd be good having you two there looking out for me.'

'Bloody Hell!' said Alec under his breath.

Tom grinned, saying, 'We can come to the cabin any time, once Alec's better. By the way, if you want to see my puppy looking *really* cute, you should see her having fun in a swimming pool. I'd love to film her paddling around, but don't know anywhere that'll allow me to take a camera into the swimming baths. If only we could hire a private pool.'

# BAD LANGUAGE

One day, when I was five years old, I overheard my sister Janet call her boyfriend a word unknown to me as I walked past her bedroom. She and Stuart were still arguing as I headed downstairs.

I waddled into the living room where my mother stood doing the ironing.

'Mummy, what does "bastard" mean?'

Mother put the iron down, shooting me that look she used to give me when I'd done something wrong, and spoke in that 'telling off' tone of voice.

'Where did you hear that word, Matthew?'

'I heard Janet say it to Stuart.'

'Did she now! Well she shouldn't have. Don't ever let me hear you say it again.'

'Why?'

'Because I said so!'

'What does it mean?'

'It's one of the worse words you can say; it's very bad.'

'Why?'

'Stop answering back and do as you're told! I said it's a bad word so don't say it.'

Mother continued ironing while I stood thinking, confused, before forgetting about it and bouncing over to my toy box to dig out my new dinosaurs.

A week later, sitting in the car with my father, I watched him change from being chatty to quiet when we became stuck in traffic. As time dragged on he started sighing and muttering. I didn't ask what was wrong, knowing that his creased brow meant not to bother him. As the traffic finally began speeding up the car stalled. Father spat out the word 'Bastard!' and shot me a guilty look. After a minute's silence he me asked what I wanted for Christmas.

Later on, at home, I toddled into the garden. Mother was giving the plants a drink. She put her watering can down when I said Father used that bad word I wasn't allowed to say.

'When did he say it? Was it while you were out today?'

'Yeah.'

'Did he now! Wait till I see him!'

'Can't grown-ups say that word either?'

'No – and you certainly can't say it!'

'I didn't! Daddy said it!'

'Well make sure you don't.'

'I won't.'

'Good. Now go and play.'

She picked up the watering can, muttering something about Father and Janet, when I remembered something else my sister said during her argument with Stuart.

'Mummy, what does "shit" mean?'

# BATS & BELLYBUTTONS

Nathan screeched his Vauxhall Astra to a halt near the kerb when he spied Kate opening her garden gate. He wound the car window down as she approached, thanking her for inviting him to her eighteenth at the village hall next weekend. Nathan was one of many teenagers whose heart throbbed when in the presence of Nubbleton's finest lady – Nubbleton being a small East Yorkshire village. What made him different to Kate's other admirers was that he stood the most chance of winning her affections. He only had one real rival, named Steven.

They hadn't been talking long when Kate's aged neighbour – Mr Floppendale – stepped outside with his Jack Russell, about to take her for a Sunday afternoon walk.

After greeting the beautiful Kate, Mr Floppendale turned to the handsome Nathan, and said, 'Have you passed your test yet?'

Nathan glanced at Kate with scrunched eyebrows. She winked at him.

'Erm, yeah, I passed last week. That's why I'm alone in my car.'

'That's good then. Anyway, must take Rum for a walk. Caahm on!'

Kate said, 'Where're you going?'

'Past the village hall, round the top road, and back here.'

'Would you mind if I joined you?'

Mr Floppendale would be glad of the company. Kate had known him all her life. He and his late wife used to treat her like their own granddaughter when she was little. She cried when Mrs Floppendale died ten years ago. Since then Kate tried to make time for him, at least once a week, hating to think of him sat lonely with just his dog to talk to.

Nathan commenced his drive to Hull, cursing the old man for interrupting his chat with the young woman.

Kate, Mr Floppendale, and Rum took a steady walk down their street. After turning a corner and passing the churchyard one of Kate's other admirers approached in his new Ford Mondeo. He didn't have the confidence to stop and talk to the glowing beauty, though he did slow down to 5 mph and wave.

Kate returned his salutation before he headed down the street opposite the church and – despite the car windows being closed and the two of them being several feet away from each other – she said, 'Hiya, John.'

Mr Floppendale heard her and said, 'Who's that?'

'John.'

'John? Is he that lad of Harpers?'

'That's right. He'll be visiting his Aunty Maria after what happened on Friday.'

'What happened?'

Kate stopped, pointing at where John had exited his car and entered a semidetached house. She explained that two days ago an escaped female prisoner had used Maria Harper's caravan to sleep in.

Mr Floppendale, in his secluded world with only little Rum to keep him company, seldom heard the local gossip.

He found this news fascinating. He stood rooted to the spot, staring at Maria's caravan, listening to Kate's tale.

'Apparently two women broke out of Everinton Prison. One was caught in that caravan, the other's still at large.'

'Ooh, I didn't know about any of this. Where did you say they'd escaped from?'

'Everinton Women's Prison.'

'Where's that?'

'Everinton.'

Everinton was a larger village than Nubbleton – perhaps a few houses short of being a town – situated four miles away.

'Did you say it was two *women* that escaped?'

'That's right. The one who slept in Maria's caravan has been caught.'

'Whose caravan is it?'

'Maria's.'

'And have they caught the other one?'

'Not yet, so remember to lock your doors tonight, Mr Floppendale.'

Minutes later, as they headed towards the village hall, they encountered Nathan's rival, Steven. He greeted Kate with a bashful smile, thanking her for inviting him to her party. He was two years Kate's senior and studied English at the University of Hull. He was now on the summer break.

As they started walking away from each other, Steven halted, turned and said, 'Stephanie told me you like foxes.'

Stephanie was Steven's younger sister.

'That's right!' said Kate, sweeping her light-brown tresses from her gorgeous face.

Colouring up, Steven related how he'd purchased a few second-hand books yesterday and accidently bought one about foxes. He was going to return it until his sister mentioned Kate's passion for these animals. Would she like it?

'Thanks, that'd be great!'

'I heard your actual birthday's before Saturday.'

'It's on Tuesday.'

'Could I give you the book then?'

'My parents are taking me out for a meal on my birthday. You could bring it round tonight though, if you've got time.'

Of course he had time.

With Kate visiting a friend in the early evening they agreed to meet at half past nine.

'Sorry to keep you waiting, Mr Floppendale – See you later, Steven!'

As they walked away Mr Floppendale said, 'Who was that?'

'Steven.'

'Is he that lad of Harpers?'

'No, you're thinking of John.'

'Who's John?'

Kate explained who was who as they walked along the top road, which was the main road passing through Nubbleton. They exited the village from one end and entered it again from the opposite side fifteen minutes later, parting company outside Mr Floppendale's house, two doors on from Kate's.


That evening Kate returned home from her friend's house quarter of an hour before Steven's arranged visit. She was about to enter her front door when a car horn beeped. With a smile, Kate released her long hair from its ponytail and strolled over to Nathan, who sat parked near the kerb, window down.

Following ten minutes of conversation, Steven walked into view from the far end of the street. Kate wasn't aware of his approach, Nathan spotted him straight away.

'Do you fancy going for a drive?'

'Thanks, but I'm expecting a visitor. Maybe another time.'

Nathan turned a violent shade of green.

'It's not Steven by any chance, is it?'

'Yes! How did you – ah!' Kate followed Nathan's eye line. 'Here's me thinking you had psychic powers!'

Kate greeted Steven with the sort of smile that could turn the most depressed hermit in the world into the equivalent of an overjoyed pauper who'd inherited a fortune from a great aunt he never knew existed. Kate had one of those glowing faces that made her appear to be smiling even when she wasn't. Her sapphire eyes sparkled like nobody else's.

Nathan's presence made Steven feel even less confident than usual. His hands shook as he handed over his gifts.

'I've brought you the book and a birthday card.'

Kate thanked Steven with warmth. She turned towards the car upon hearing a door click open.

Nathan stepped out, standing taller than Steven by a few inches. He'd left school aged sixteen to commence work in the building trade, resulting in him developing broad shoulders and stocky build.

Steven was no runt either, though with his time devoted to studies, he didn't get as much opportunity for exercise as he'd like, though he still possessed an impressive physique. He owned the most handsome face of the two rivals.

Nathan opened the rear driver door announcing that he too had bought Kate a present and card. He'd been all the way to Hull to get them.

Steven reddened at this proclamation, blushing more so upon seeing the giant card and glitter bag that Nathan passed to Kate. He looked away as his rival shot him a smug look. The tiny card and second-hand book about foxes – not even wrapped – paled compared to this.

Nathan said, 'Why don't I take this inside while you carry his little lot?'

With a defeated smile, Steven said, 'I'll leave you to it. See you at the party.'

'Hang on! You can both come in! My parents won't be back from their meal for another hour. You can stay until they come home.'

Steven was about to reply when Mr Floppendale stepped outside, calling Kate's name. Did she know how to retune his Freeview TV set? He'd tried updating it and lost all of his channels.

Steven said, 'I'll sort it for him.'

As he jogged over to Mr Floppendale, Kate told him to come round afterwards. Steven nodded and smiled before disappearing inside.

Nathan smirked to himself as he alone followed the dazzling Kate indoors.

The living room was of medium proportions. A matching three-piece suite in green complemented the wallpaper and soft carpet. The place was dust-free, smelling of scented vanilla.

Kate placed her gifts on the couch middle seat. She sat at one side, Nathan the other. As he relaxed back, sitting with his knees miles apart, Kate wondered if he stored a cactus in his pants. He in turn wondered how her ultra-tight jeans didn't split when she crossed her shapely legs, imagining it must take her half an hour to pull them on ... and off.

Although her birthday was in two days' time she opened his present now: it was a huge box of chocolates. She smiled, thanking him. Of course she was grateful but the book on foxes was the better gift. Kate led a healthy lifestyle, involving little in the way of chocolate consumption. Still, they'd last her a long time with her rule of one 'cheat meal' per week when she'd eat whatever she liked.

Nathan leant forward, his expression serious. Could

he accompany Kate to her eighteenth at the village hall on Saturday as her boyfriend? His eyes didn't leave her face as he waited for an answer.

Kate saw how confident this stocky young man was. They didn't have much in common, yet he was decisive, respectful, owned a car, and had great shoulders.

'Tell you what; let's treat my eighteenth as a first date. If we feel we're compatible, let's go out a few more times. If by then we still don't hate each other I'd love to make us an official item.'

'I say we make your eighteenth our *second* date. Let this be the first.'

Kate nodded, shooting him a sparkling smile.

Nathan said, 'In that case we don't want that bloody Steven interrupting us.'

Kate's face dropped. She'd forgotten about Steven.

'I've invited him here. I can't tell –'

'Don't tell him anything. Leave him knocking when he calls.'

'I can't do that!'

'Put some music on. We won't hear him knock, but he'll hear the music, realising –'

'Okay, seeing as I've promised you a date and we've only got an hour; less if my parents come home early. They won't be impressed finding us down here with music blasting out. We'll go to my room.'

Nathan had no problem with this arrangement. He followed Kate upstairs with eyes transfixed by her bottom straining against her jeans.

Strolling across the narrow landing, he said, 'Why's that got a bolt on it?'

He alluded to the smallest door of three bedrooms, currently ajar. Kate explained that when her older brother – now away at Lincoln University – was little he sometimes sleepwalked. Their father was concerned his son may fall downstairs during one of these night-time wanderings, hence the bolt.

'My dad's just never got round to removing it,' she said, leading Nathan into her room.

Kate shut the door and window, followed by drawing the curtains and flicking on the light, as dusk was settling. She dragged her chair out from under the dressing table, offering it to Nathan. He thanked her, sitting down with his knees stretching further apart than before, making Kate think he really did keep something sharp in his underwear. She kept her little hi-fi on a shelf, while the speakers were attached to wall brackets, facing her single bed at the opposite side of the room. She switched the stereo on at the wall.

With a twinge of guilt, thinking of Steven as the standby button came on, she asked Nathan if he wanted a radio station on or if he'd rather choose a CD.

'Put anything on; quickly, before that prat gets here!'

Kate stood facing him, arms folded.

'I'm liking this arrangement less and less. Steven's not a —'

'Shit!' Nathan jumped to his feet. 'What was that noise?'

'What noise?'

Nathan clutched her arm, telling her to listen.

'Something's tapping!'

Kate strolled over to the wall parting them from her brother's old bedroom. Yes, a tapping noise was evident, like someone lightly hitting the wall with their fingertips.

She faced Nathan, mirroring his anxious countenance, whispering that the big window would be open in her brother's room.

'I doubt anyone could climb up and get in unless …'

'Unless what!'

'Unless they were desperate, like someone on the run from the law.'

Nathan had heard the news of the escaped prisoners and required no elaboration. He took his mobile from his pocket to call the police. No reception.

'I can never get a signal on my phone in here either. If –' Kate paused, hearing the light tapping sound again. When it ceased she continued. 'If we wait here we could get cornered. The top step creaks. She'll hear if we try escaping. We'll have to try locking her in. Let's hope she doesn't reach the door before us.'

'I heard she's a huge woman with a history of violence. She's likely to use the nearest object to bludgeon us with, assuming she's not already armed. Have you anything we can use for a weapon?'

Kate picked up a hard-backed hairbrush from the dressing table.

'This'll sting a little.'

'You keep hold of that. If she charges out of the room I'll grab her arms while you whack her head with it.'

Kate turned the handle without making a sound. She eased her door wide open, exchanging a concerned glance with Nathan. No noises came from the other bedroom.

They sprang onto the landing. At the same time a gust of wind forced Kate's brother's bedroom door to swing wide open. The sudden movement caused the pair to freeze. In a panic, they both ran forward to bolt the door, colliding into each other. Nathan's bulky weight rocked Kate's balance, sending her fumbling a couple of paces before landing flat on her face; her upper body lying in the bedroom. The hairbrush flew from her hand, skidding across the floor.

Nathan stepped into the room to help Kate up. Only when she stood beside him did they both realise that no one else was present.

The room contained a single bed and a built-in wardrobe. The foot of the bed faced the door. This was where Kate parked her bottom, placed a hand to her heaving bosom, and emitted a relieved giggle.

Nathan stood looking down at her, releasing a nervous laugh. He thought now would be a good time to take Kate in his arms and kiss her. He took a step forward.

She met his gaze whilst pointing at the window, asking if he minded shutting it and drawing the curtains. As he turned his head towards the window something caught his eye – something on the curtain. He took one step closer, squinting his eyes. The room was darkish. The light spilling from Kate's open bedroom door was the only source of illumination.

'Aarrgghh!'

Nathan's outburst was caused by his discerning the identity of the 'something' on the curtain: it was a bat.

Nathan's scream scared the creature even more than he frightened Kate. The bat started flapping around. Nathan screamed once more, turned on his heel, leaped through the open doorway, turned, slammed the door behind him, and bolted it shut.

Kate shouted for him to let her out. The bat fluttered around behind her.

'I'll get help!' said Nathan, charging across the landing. 'I can't be in the same house as that *thing*! You'll be okay but it'll come after me!'

Kate pounded on the door as Nathan thundered down the staircase. She switched the light on and faced the bat. Eventually it hung upside down on the curtain again. Unlike Nathan, Kate didn't have chiroptophobia but that didn't mean she wanted a bat for a roommate. She decided to sit on the bed until her parents arrived home. They should be forty minutes or so.

Quarter of an hour later she heard heavy footsteps on the stairs. Kate jumped up, glad that her parents were back early.

'Dad! I'm locked inside the little bedroom!' She heard the top step creak, but no reply followed her call. 'Dad?'

The bolt slid open. The handle turned. The door opened.

A woman built like a grizzly entered the room. Her face looked like it'd been washed with detergent, scrubbed with wire wool, and dried with nettle leaves. With a twisted nose, eyes like a weasel's, and a mouth like a vulture's beak, she wasn't going to become a future contender for Miss World.

'My, my! What have we here? Been scaring your fellah away, eh? Just seen him shoot out the house, leaving the door open for me.'

Kate – her full breasts rising up and down like she was on a bouncy castle – backed up against the far wall.

'My parents will be home *any minute*!'

'Is that right?' The ugly woman held up the largest of Kate's mother's kitchen knives. 'I'm willing to take my chances. When I was inside there were no sweet things like you to amuse me. Strip naked! Keep your back to me at all times. Don't turn round even for a second. I'll cut a sash out of one of the curtains, wide enough for you to tie round your waist and cover your stomach.'

Kate faced the wall. After removing her top, she half turned, dropping it on the floor.

'Keep your front to the bloody wall!'

The woman's exclamation proved loud enough to disturb the bat. Now it startled her.

Her instinct was to slash when the bat almost collided into her face. The surprise forced her to step back, slip on Kate's hairbrush, and land on her backside.

Kate's best escape route was over the bed. She leapt upon it, tumbled over the end, and crashed onto the floor. Like earlier, she lay half in, half out of the room, only this time her legs remained in the room.

Both women simultaneously gained their feet. The criminal's eyes widened as they fell on Kate's flat stomach. She screamed and threw the knife at her. Luckily for Kate, the aim was taken by a shaky arm. The knife handle skimmed her hip on its flight past.

Kate charged at the door, determined to bolt it. At the same time the criminal – with wide eyes still glaring at Kate's bare stomach – shrieked again: *she* slammed the door shut.

Kate – perplexed yet in control – slid the bolt across before charging downstairs. She dashed into the hallway, flicked the light on, and collided into someone previously hidden by the darkness. She was about to scream but sighed with relief instead, embracing Steven, speaking in a language he didn't understand.

'Slow down! I can't catch what you're saying!'

She stepped back, pointing upstairs, trying to make herself clear. All was quiet up above now.

Suddenly the front door opened. Kate jumped into Steven's arms, gripping him tight, only to let go of him as if she'd scolded herself when her parents entered the building, discovering their daughter – and her choice of bra – hugging a young man.

Steven had been so concerned for Kate that it took this embarrassing moment for him to notice her ample breasts heaving in their lacy attire.

Steven had entered the building just before Kate's flight from danger despite no one answering his knock. When he was helping Mr Floppendale he saw Nathan drive past the window as though he was being pursued by the law. He wondered if Kate was upset after having an argument and needed a friend.

Kate's parents soon realised their daughter and Steven were not the homecoming present they had to deal with when a loud thud outside caught everyone's attention.

In the criminal's desperation to escape she tried leaving via the bedroom window. Needless to say, the loud thud was her falling to her death.


When the police arrived everyone sat in the living room answering questions. Kate sat between her mother and Steven on the couch. They learned that the criminal suffered from omphalophobia.

Kate forgave Nathan for abandoning her, as she understood what it felt like having an irrational fear. Ever since she watched one of the many adaptations of *A Christmas Carol* when she was a little girl she'd been unnerved by door knockers with carved faces. Even so, she no longer had as much time for Nathan as before.

A fortnight after Kate turned eighteen she asked Steven to be her boyfriend. Despite them going on several dates, giving him signals that she was interested, he was just too nervous to make the first move. Only when Steven kissed his dream girl properly for the first time did his confidence grow.

The bat, incidentally, flew out of the window after the criminal made her exit and went on to lead a happy life.

# RISING AROMAS

Takamasa stood in his store doorway gazing at passers-by on a sunny morning. Twenty years ago he left Japan to set up his aromatherapy business in New York City.

Today he observed two potential customers peering through the shop window. A tall man in need of a haircut was accompanied by a beautiful blonde wearing a summery dress.

The hyperactive Takamasa approached them, smiling and nodding.

'Greetings to you both! How can I be of service?'

'We're only looking,' said the man.

'Wonderful!' Takamasa rubbed his hands together. 'Come into my humble establishment! See the amazing products I have on offer!'

'We ain't got time.'

'We can spare a few minutes, Casey,' said the woman.

'Wonderful!' said Takamasa with a beaming smile. 'Come in, come in, come in!'

Takamasa had an irregular twitch in his right eye. Casey discovered this when they entered the store.

'Natalie, that guy just *winked* at me! Let's go.'

'You're imagining things. I'll just have a quick look

around.'

Casey cleared his throat, about to speak, when Takamasa interrupted.

'Sounds like you have the flu, sir, or perhaps you suffer with asthma? Or is it whooping cough?'

'What the hell are you talking about?' said Casey, after clearing his throat again.

'Ah, it seems you just have the common cold. No problem. I have remedies for everything, big or small. Excuse me for one moment.'

Takamasa walked behind the main counter.

Casey turned open-mouthed towards Natalie. She was too busy examining the herbs on the shelves to notice his raised-eyebrows expression.

Takamasa returned, saying, 'I have found a treatment for your cold, sir.'

'I don't –'

'In fact there are several remedies at your disposal. Eucalyptus and lemon are excellent for reducing cold symptoms.'

Casey put his hands on the sides of his head, groaning.

'Let's go before I strangle this guy.'

'Calm down, he's only being helpful.'

Casey's brow furrowed when Takamasa 'winked' at him again.

'Quite often, sir, mental conditions like stress or depression can cause illnesses like yours. Perhaps you would care to try Bergamot oil? It contains a strong antidepressant and relieves stress.'

Casey clenched his fists.

'I am *not* stressed or depressed, damn it!'

'Oh dear.' Takamasa's smile vanished. 'I think we should begin with a head massage before trying anything else. I will call for my assistant. Wazuka!'

A broad grin decorated Takamasa's face again. Casey turned to Natalie, running his fingers through his mop of hair, but she was still distracted by the products on display.

He faced Takamasa again, shaking a finger at him.

'Listen, buddy. I do *not* need any damn remedies and I'll be *damned* if I need a …'

The beautiful Wazuka entered the room just as Takamasa's eye twitched at Casey.

'Ah, Wazuka! Yes! Yes! Take this gentleman to Massage Room Number 2. He has a cold and suffers from stress and depression.'

Casey smiled at the shapely Japanese woman before asking Natalie if he had time for a head massage. Yes, it was fine. She was enjoying browsing the store.

As Wazuka led Casey away, Takamasa approached Natalie.

'Do you suffer from stress as well, madam?'

'Not really. I often play tennis and my shoulders feel sore from yesterday's match.'

'Ah yes!' said Takamasa, nodding. 'Even professional tennis players have these problems when they pass thirty.'

'I'm *twenty-four*!'

'Ha, ha! Very good, madam! Now let me see. Marjoram is effective for relieving tiredness, along with soothing the muscles. This will help ease your shoulders. A thorough massage is also required. Please come with me to Massage Room Number 1.'

Takamasa's right eye twitched as he finished his sentence.

'I'll wait for your assistant, if you don't mind.'

'I do not mind at all, madam. I am happy to massage you.'

'Thanks, but I'll wait for the lady.'

'Nonsense, madam. Wazuka will be a long time. Your friend's cold and stress levels will need much work. Allow me to gather some bottles of my best oils before taking you into Massage Room Number 1.'

'I'm not sure. Anyway, don't you need to keep an eye on the shop? What if someone comes in?'

'If anyone comes through the front door a bell will ring in every room and Wazuka will answer it. Be assured that I will not leave you alone.'

Natalie followed Takamasa into the long massage room. A table and a chair were situated at one end, several cabinets filled with oils were fitted to the back wall, and two cupboards stood at the other end. Takamasa arranged his oils on the worktop, while Natalie sat waiting on the chair.

Takamasa, nodding and smiling, said, 'Please get undressed, madam.'

'Undressed? Can't you massage me with my dress on?'

Natalie plucked at the narrow fabric covering the centre of her shoulder. Surely all she needed to do was slip the straps down her arms an inch or two?

'To receive the full benefit, madam, you must strip to your underwear.'

Takamasa's eye twitched. Natalie folded her arms.

'I don't see why that's necessary.'

'Madam, my experienced hands will be able to perform at their best if you are undressed. Please strip to your underwear and lay face down on the table. This way I can perform a more intense massage of your shoulders, back, and legs.'

'My back and legs!'

'Of course, madam.'

'My back and legs are fine. I just need –'

'Your shoulders massaging, yes, but these aches and pains will spread. The discomfort in your shoulders today will soon pass through your body, down to your feet –'

'My feet? How –'

'Yes, madam, your feet. You should have regular full-body massages if you intend to carry on playing so much tennis at your age. If you do not take care of your body now you will get gout within the next ten years.'

'Gout? From aching shoulders?'

Takamasa assured Natalie that her health was at risk. At length his persistence convinced her that she'd contract several illnesses before turning forty if she refused the full treatment.

After removing her shoes and dress, Natalie's face reddened as she stood wearing only lacy underwear, while Takamasa looked her up and down, nodding and smiling.

'You have the figure of an elegant tennis player, madam. You must be six feet tall.'

'I'm five nine. Now can we get on with this?'

'Of course, madam. Please mount the table. I may be shorter than you, but have strong hands and know what to do with them, as you will find out. I will mix Marjoram and Rosemary together and give you an intense rub-down.'

Takamasa gave Natalie two large towels to use as a pillow as she didn't want to put her face into the hole at the end of the table. She settled on her stomach; her head resting on one side.

Takamasa draped a towel across Natalie's bottom. He spent time patting it down. At length Natalie raised herself on her forearms, craning her neck, looking back.

'What are you doing?'

'Making sure the towel does not slip off, madam.'

She assured him the towel was firmly in place before lying down again.

Takamasa poured a drop of oil onto a handkerchief and placed it near Natalie's nose.

'Sniff this please, madam.'

'What is it?'

'A special Jasmine mix. Have another drop.'

Natalie inhaled the fragrance.

'Mmmm! That's lovely!'

She closed her eyes, starting to relax, listening to Takamasa singing an uptempo Japanese song as he began massaging her shoulders. When he moved on to her back, Natalie asked what the Jasmine mix did.

'It enhances mental alertness, amongst other things,

madam.'

'What other things?'

'Here are more drops for you to inhale.'

Takamasa resumed his joyful singing, which became more cheerful when he began massaging Natalie's toned calves.

She lay with a contented expression on her face, breathing in the strong scent.

'This Jasmine mix is wonderful. I hope I won't overdose on it.'

'Ha, ha! Very funny, madam!'

Takamasa's singing became even louder when he moved on to Natalie's thighs, until he suddenly fell silent, stepping back from the table.

'There is an intruder on your leg, madam.'

'An intruder? What do you mean?'

Natalie elevated her head, watching Takamasa walk towards the cupboards at the far end of the room.

'Please, madam,' he said, walking back, raising a hand, nodding and smiling, 'lay down. I will soon sort out this little problem.'

'What problem?'

Takamasa told Natalie to brace herself before resuming his happy Japanese song.

'Brace myself for what?' She propped herself up on her elbows. 'What are you – Ouch!'

Takamasa showed Natalie a pair of tweezers gripping the hair he'd plucked from her thigh.

'You missed one, madam. It is very blonde. No one would have noticed it, but I know you want your legs to be perfectly smooth. There is no need to thank me.'

'*Thank* you?'

'Ah, my pleasure, madam. I require no extra charge for removing the hair.'

Natalie slid off the table as Casey knocked on the door before entering.

'Wait, madam. If you stop before the treatment is

complete you will not fully benefit from it. Inhale more Jasmine and please remount the table.'

Takamasa held out the bottle.

'I think I've inhaled enough.'

'Jasmine?' said Casey. 'Ain't that an aphrodisiac?'

'Amongst other things, sir.'

'Amongst other things indeed!' said Natalie, swiping the bottle from his hand, passing it to her boyfriend. 'As soon as I'm dressed we're leaving.'

Casey sniffed the bottle.

'There ain't just Jasmine in this. What else have you put in here, buddy?'

'It is mixed with a popular ingredient, imported from Japan. It enhances certain properties of the Jasmine.'

'I think I know *which* properties!' said Natalie, feeling her passions rise.

Casey pocketed the bottle.

Takamasa turned to Natalie, who sat replacing her shoes.

'If you stay I will only charge for what I have done so far and will finish the massage at no extra cost.'

'Better still, how does you not charging anything and me not mentioning your special "mixture" to anyone sound? And don't get me started on that hair-plucking incident!'

Casey paid for his treatment and passed Wazuka a generous tip on the way out. Natalie refused to pay anything.

Once they'd gone, Wazuka observed Takamasa's face droop. After swearing in Japanese, he removed his hat and threw it in the air. When it landed he jumped up and down on it several times. He stood quiet for a moment before retrieving his hat, dusting it down, and replacing it on his head.

Takamasa's cheerful smile reappeared when a young couple entered the store.

# THE DARK HANDER

Jerry entered The Wooden Spoon pub during a warm August evening. He didn't usually spend his Saturday nights in the village, but learning that Monika – a Polish beauty – worked weekends here, glass collecting, he decided to have a change from the norm.

Jerry first met Monika in the local post office. They chatted whilst queuing. She mentioned being new to the village and had recently begun a weekend job at The Wooden Spoon. Her smile and Slavic eyes took Jerry's breath away.

Jerry, aged twenty-four, was the youngest punter in the half-full pub. This was one of two drinking holes in the village of Skrewfoek. The other stood at the opposite side of the road.

Standing with his back to a wall, pint of lager in hand, he felt a rush of nerves sweep through his body as Monika appeared from the kitchen, heading towards him, wearing an enrapturing smile and a summery dress, leaving him gaping at the sight of this brunette goddess.

She said hello, leaning towards him, the big smile still radiating. As her cheek neared his, he kissed it, remembering that another Polish woman he once knew always greeted him this way. However, Monika was only leaning forward to take an empty glass from the shelf behind him.

She stepped back, still smiling, saying, 'I speak with you later.'

She strolled off with the glass, leaving Jerry searching for a hole to jump into it. Yes, he felt happy to kiss that beautiful cheek, but he only did so thinking she was offering it to him. As time ticked on he knew he'd have to find the courage to ask her to join him for a drink after her shift. She seemed to like him. And why not? He was no poor catch with his handsome features and designer clothes.

Jerry strategically left his empty glasses on the shelf behind him throughout the evening. As Monika collected one of his previous vessels, at quarter to eleven, he asked when she finished work.

'In about ten minute. Why? How long you staying here?' Before Jerry could answer, she added, 'Will you take me home?'

In a high-pitched squeak he answered yes. This was a positive step, albeit a quick step. He asked her if she fancied joining him in the other pub after finishing her shift, rather than heading off immediately. Monika thanked him, but declined, for she was short of money.

When Jerry offered to buy her a couple of drinks, she said, 'You are kind, but I am not ... how did my friend say this? Ah! I am not spongy.'

'Let me just buy you *one* drink, then. That won't make you a sponger.'

'Hmmm ... All right, but you must let me get you one another time. Okay?'

Of course it was okay. She was arranging a second date before having their first.

Once Monika finished her shift, she accompanied Jerry to the other pub, namely The Upturned Table, persuading him to try a double vodka with cola. She downed hers in one, encouraging him to follow suit. Even though he hated vodka he managed to conceal a shudder after emptying his glass. Jerry's hopes of spending half an hour sitting in a corner, chatting with this stunning Polish lady, had been reduced to a two-minute wait to get served, followed by ten seconds in making their drinks disappear. Now the pressure of walking her home without as much Dutch courage as he would have preferred weighed on his mind.

Monika's English was good, though far from perfect. Jerry believed that if a woman asks a man to *take* her home she wants him to spend the night. To *walk* a lady home means stopping at their door and either passing the threshold together or saying goodnight. If Monika intended to invite him in to share her bed their encounter may be labelled as a one night stand. Jerry would usually consider this a good outcome. Relationships weren't his thing but Monika's angelic appearance and warm personality affected him in a way he couldn't describe. For the first time ever he'd met someone he wanted to have a steady relationship with.

Stepping out of the pub, Jerry asked Monika where she lived.

'You know where is Yeoman House?'

Jerry nodded, staring with raised eyebrows.

'Ha, ha! You look surprise! You think I own this big house? Ha, ha! No, no, no! I am au pair to the Vermonts' children. I would not be working in a pub if I was rich.'

Jerry moved to the village five months ago, having previously lived near Hull. He knew names and places in Skrewfoek, yet couldn't always put them together. He'd driven past Yeoman House many times. This large building was viewable from a main road. He learned of the Vermonts' wealth after seeing them dining in The Wooden Spoon one Sunday afternoon. The barmaid gave him an overview of who they were though didn't mention they resided in Yeoman House.

Several minutes later, near the other end of the village, Monika stopped, pointing at the field on the opposite side of the road.

'We will take a quick cut through here. It take too long walking round.'

Jerry looked across at the blackened field. Cows frequented this area during the day, though now the only sound was the rustle of trees. Jerry felt a creepy ambience rush over him as they neared the stile.

Pointing at Monika's sandals, he said, 'Will you be all right in those?'

'Yes, the track is dry. You go first then help me over, okay?'

'What about thistles or nettles?'

Monika placed dainty hands on rounded hips, tilting her head to one side.

'I do not understand.'

Jerry explained his meaning, stating that her unprotected feet – and possibly her legs in that short dress – may get stung by protruding nettles or thistles hiding in the dark.

'Ah ha! You mean those stingy plant-things!' She waved her hand like she was swatting a fly. 'Is okay. I walk this way many time. Nothing stingy ever hurt me.'

Jerry glanced at the open field with all its black eeriness. He turned back, charmed by that beaming face, beckoning him to climb over the stile. With reluctance, he did so. With no reluctance he took Monika's hand as she stepped over – not that she needed any help. She must've wanted him to take her hand.

The field dipped before rising again at the halfway stage. Reaching this juncture, Jerry heard a sighing sound. He grasped Monika's bare arm, whispering that he'd heard something odd. They stared ahead. A shape was apparent; something on all fours. Was it a wandering cow? No, it wasn't big enough. A large dog, perhaps?

Jerry recalled a time recently spent in The Upturned

Table when several punters swore they'd seen a beast wandering across Grafton Field. One man believed it to be the ghost of a dog who haunted this area after being trampled to death by cows. A middle-aged couple related how their young son declared spotting a tiger in the field during a school nature walk. An elderly woman swore blind it was a rabcat; a freak of nature, born of a male rabbit and a female domestic cat. The general opinion was that a wealthy villager had bought an exotic pet – a panther – but one night they forgot to lock its cage. Ever since, some have believed that the black cat stalks the fields surrounding Skrewfoek, occasionally slinking into Grafton Field on moonless nights like this.

The memory of these suppositions flooded back into Jerry's mind. A wealthy villager with expensive tastes. Who better than the Vermonts in their out-of-the-way abode to purchase an exotic pet? Perhaps the wandering panther considers this area as its territory, maybe hoping to devour the Vermonts in revenge for keeping it caged.

Jerry whispered, 'Let's turn back.'

'Why? It –'

'Shhh! It might hear! Let's go!'

'Is okay. Come!'

Monika took a firm grip of Jerry's hand before setting off towards the mysterious four-legged creature in the darkness.

Jerry's heart rocketed like a cheetah after consuming a bucketful of stimulant drink. They'd barely walked three feet when Jerry halted, gripping Monika's hand tighter, as 'the thing' rose on its hind legs.

'Is okay, Jerry! I know this man.'

Man? Surely not. This huge shape in the dark was more like a bear.

Monika egged Jerry to keep moving before speaking to the ominous figure.

'Hello, Mr Douglas! You are smelling the cow mess again?'

Jerry's fear gave way to puzzlement. A bulky middle-aged man, bald and bearded with a towel around his neck, stood before them.

'Jerry, do you know Mr Douglas?'

No, he'd never had the pleasure.

Mr Douglas noticed Monika's hand entwined with Jerry's and said, 'Guess you won't need me to walk you to Yeoman House tonight?'

No, she only needed one escort.

'No probs. I'll get back to it. See you about.'

Jerry couldn't resist asking what Mr Douglas was getting back to.

'Cowpat sniffing,' he said. 'Ever tried it?'

Jerry had never heard of such a pastime. He gazed in wonder as Mr Douglas pottered over to the nearest cowpat, knelt down on all fours, draped the towel over his head, and proceeded to sniff the former contents of a cow's innards.

Monika looked at Jerry, giggling, before suggesting they get moving.

'So does that guy usually walk you home after your weekend shifts?'

'Only if he is smelling the cow mess along my path. We do not arrange anything. Sometimes I get scared going down the track to the house. This is why I am glad you are taking me tonight – but not just because of The Dark Hander. I really like –'

'The Dark Hander?'

'Yes. Sometimes I hear him near the track. I do not want to meet him at night.'

Jerry gulped before asking what this Dark Hander was like during the day.

'I do not know. We never meet but I hear him at night.'

Monika released Jerry's hand when nearing the stile. She took it again as he helped her over and kept hold when they crossed the main road – empty of traffic at this hour – onto the grass bank at the opposite side.

They heard a rustling noise about halfway between where they began walking along the bank and the turn-off to the Vermonts' track up ahead. Large hedges rose on their right, with nothing but open fields behind them. Stories of panthers, spectral dogs, and rabcats flooded back into Jerry's thoughts as the rustling grew louder. Monika didn't ease his mind by telling him to walk faster.

'It might be The Dark Hander! I do not want to see him!'

Neither did Jerry.

They were almost at the end of the bank when the sound of something emerging from a gap in the hedge caused them to turn their heads.

Having froze in terror, they both sighed with relief as a seventy-something woman, raising a branch in one hand, wished them good evening.

Monika asked if she was okay.

'Aye, don't worry about me, pet. I had to get out of bed; couldn't sleep, remembering walking past here this aft. We had an argument, you see.' She raised the branch. 'I threw my stick over the hedge cos she ruffled my feathers, saying I'd forgotten to bring the washing in when I knew full well I did.' She shuffled across the road, looking at the branch, saying, 'I'll be able to sleep now, now that we're friends again.'

Turning down the Vermonts' track, Jerry remarked that there were some unusual people living in Skrewfoek.

Monika said, 'At least they are harmless ... except The Dark Hander.'

Jerry's stomach tightened as they continued down the gravel track.

After two minutes or so the Vermonts' big house could be discerned in the blackness. All lights were out.

'Looks like everyone's in bed.'

'They are away with the children this weekend. I will be glad when they come back. The Dark Hander scares me when he shoots his gun.'

'His gun!'

'Yes, he – what was that!'

'What!'

They stood still, squeezing hands. Jerry sighed, assuring Monika it was only ducks on the stream running alongside the back of the house.

'If this is so, we should hurry! Where they are, The Dark Hander will be near!'

As they hastened on in silence, Jerry's cogs started ticking.

Approaching the front door, Monika produced the keys from her bag; dropping them when a loud noise erupted from the silence.

She clasped Jerry's arms, with face aghast, and said, 'The Dark Hander has just shot dead a dack! Listen!'

The ducks had become more vocal.

When the sound had boomed-out a change took place in Jerry that nearly altered the dry conditions of his underwear. Yet now, after listening to the quacking ducks and Monika's pronunciation of the aforementioned birds, the truth revealed itself: dark hander … dack hunder … duck hunter – The Duck Hunter!

Jerry smiled, aware that no one would be hunting anything on the Vermonts' property. He was poised to explain that the sound was only a device farmers use to scare birds off their fields until Monika said something to change his mind.

'Please do not leave me here alone. I do not trust The Dark Hander with his gun. Will you come inside with me?'

'Only if my being here won't get you into trouble with the Vermonts.'

'They will not return till Monday morning. Will you come in?'

Naturally he would.

They entered a kitchen the same size as Jerry's living room and sat facing each other at the same side of a large oak table. After talking until midnight Monika declared she was ready for bed, informing Jerry he could sleep in the room adjacent to hers.

They ambled together, arms around each other, through the huge house, up the wide staircase, across a landing that stretched further than Jerry's back yard, and stopped outside a bedroom door. They kissed each other on the cheek before saying goodnight.

Boom!

The distant noise prompted Monika to press her hands to her chest like an Egyptian mummy.

'He is still out there!'

Jerry felt a pang of guilt, observing the worry etched on Monika's face. He should explain that nobody was shooting ducks or even firing a gun.

Before he could ease her mind, she said, 'I do not know why tonight I am such the scaredy-cow, but I feel worried to be alone in my room. Will you sleep with me?'

Occasionally that evening Jerry had misunderstood something Monika had said, thus prompting him to ask her to repeat herself. This time he understood perfectly, yet still asked what she' just said. Monika obliged, causing his face to adopt a tomato-coloured glow.

'If you feel embarrass about taking away your clothes, do not worry, I will turn out the light first. So you will sleep with me?'

'I'll just go for a – where's the bathroom?'

Jerry pottered down the long landing, turned left, sauntered a few more paces, and closed the bathroom door behind him. Was it possible that she *literally* wanted him to sleep with her? Surely this type of arrangement between a man and woman who'd only met once before was impossible without leading to sex. Such an experience with this goddess would be a good thing – a great thing – but Jerry feared that a one night stand would result in her avoiding him afterwards. There may be an awkward hello, an embarrassed smile, but nothing more according to his experiences of one-offs with women he'd met once or twice. Yet she did tell him lots of personal things during their chat in the kitchen. He could only hope that if they did become intimate she wouldn't avoid him afterwards and hopefully become his girlfriend in time.

Jerry switched his mobile off before entering the bedroom. Monika – now attired in a nightie that didn't quite hide her skimpy knickers – stood hanging her dress up in a wardrobe near the foot of a single bed.

'I will turn off the light for you.' She looked beyond Jerry's shoulder, adding, 'Is one pillow okay?'

He turned round. The room contained two single beds. He'd been oblivious to this second one. Monika's present attire may have had something to do with this oversight.

She turned the light out. Jerry could still discern her well-formed silhouette in the blackness. He wondered whilst undressing if she could make-out his muscular physique, and if so, did he appeal to her as much as she did to him? He stripped down to his boxer shorts before climbing on the bed. As his eyes adjusted to the dark, Monika's perfect shape became easier to distinguish. She lay on her side on top of the covers, propping her head up on her elbow. He did the same as she began talking, wondering whether she'd scoot over to his bed if another boom shattered the silence. Instead she became drowsy and said goodnight.

Jerry listened to the sound of her breathing slow down. She dropped off in about ten minutes. He, however, managed ten minutes of broken sleep over the subsequent few hours. At length he could take no more of this maddening situation. All remained quiet outside. No loud noises were likely to scare his sleeping angel. He may as well go home and rest.

Once dressed, Jerry stole from the room, down to the kitchen. Having found a pen and Post-it notes he scribbled a message for Monika explaining he needed to go but didn't want to wake her. He also left his mobile number.

Jerry found a key for the back door. He mentioned in his note that he'd post this through the letterbox.

He opened the door. Dawn was breaking on another warm August day. The kitchen light behind him reached far enough to distinguish two dead ducks lying several feet from the step. He shuffled towards them, eyes darting in every direction.

Trees and high hedges bordered this impressive back garden. A large garage stood about twenty feet away on his far right. The stream — with fewer ducks floating on it than last night — was further back still, running the full length of the Vermonts' property, emerging from one bridge on Jerry's right, disappearing under another to his left.

With no one evident in the semi-darkness, Jerry returned his attention to the dead birds, nudging them with his foot, hoping to decipher whether they'd been shot. Even with the kitchen light seeping out behind him it wasn't bright enough to reveal the cause of death. Could Monika be right after all? Was there really a duck hunter? If so, why would a poacher leave their kill near someone else's doorstep?

Thinking Monika would be perturbed if she stepped outside, finding two dead bodies waiting to greet her, Jerry decided to get rid of them. He closed the back door without locking it, intending to return to wash his hands after moving the bodies. He grabbed each bird by their wings and dragged them towards the large garage.

After walking round the front end Jerry wandered a few more paces before dropping the ducks against the wall. Whilst checking his hands for blood, a noise caught his ear — a human snore coming from the far end of the garage wall. In the receding traces of night Jerry detected a man-sized shape lying asleep.

He crept over to the slumbering figure. He gazed down on a bearded man aged about fifty, lying on his side, wearing dark clothes and a peaked cap. Jerry blinked when a sudden gust of wind blew a feather in his face — a duck feather that had wafted up from the sleeping man.

He held his breath upon noticing the man's hands: one was the same white flesh-colour as his own; the other appeared black. A gap between the shirt cuff and hand revealed a glimpse of wrist — white wrist.

'The Dark Hander!'

The words fell out of Jerry's mouth without him realising it. He hadn't spoken in a whisper either. He stepped back as the sleeping man slept no more.

Intense eyes opened like a demon from a horror film.

Jerry observed a large cylindrical mark below the man's left orb — a *dark* patch on his cheek. What's more, the eye above this cheek appeared bulgy in a strange way. All these defects were on the man's left side. Daylight had not fully arrived but Jerry could see these distinguishing marks well enough to know that this was The Dark Hander. With such crazy people living in Skrewfoek, with their bizarre activities and superstitions, Jerry had to get himself and Monika away from here.

The man sat up in a sudden movement.

Jerry sprinted off in a quicker movement. He hurtled towards the back door, shot inside, locked himself in, fell over a chair, got up, bolted towards and up the stairs, tripped over the final step, picked himself up, rocketed towards his former bedroom and barged inside.

Monika had just swung her legs out of bed as Jerry burst into the room. Now she was the one having difficulty understanding him. All she could grasp was that The Dark Hander lay behind his anxiety. She made him sit beside her on the bed, taking his hand in both of hers and, speaking in soft tones, asked him to explain clearly what had happened. Once she understood, Monika asked Jerry to phone the police.

An hour later they sat together at the kitchen table,

accompanied by PC Harrison.

Monika asked what had become of The Dark Hander.

The officer explained that the man Jerry encountered is well known to most of Skrewfoek's residents. His real name is Jacob Gothleplot. He tramps between this village and the ones either side of it. Having questioned Mr Gothleplot, PC Harrison related to Jerry and Monika what happened.

Jacob Gothleplot had been traipsing across the fields during the afternoon, heading towards the Vermonts' property. He'd been plodding close to the hedge when, out of the blue, a five-foot branch came hurtling over the greenery, landing end-first on his cheek, thus explaining the cylindrical mark beneath his eye. The shock of the impact from this flying branch caused Mr Gothleplot to tumble over. He banged his head on the only large stone in the massive field, rendering himself unconscious. When he recovered he still felt dizzy, resulting in him falling the other way, almost into the hedge. This time he landed face first on a nettle, causing his eye to swell up. He also cut his left palm on a broken bottle.

He got up again, changing his course in favour of Skrewfoek Vicarage, where he knew he'd be welcome for a short period. The vicar tended Mr Gothleplot's wounds, giving him a large plaster for his palm. Realising this may come off during various undertakings the vicar gave him a black leather glove to wear. He only had a left glove as the right one had been stolen by a naughty puppy.

Jacob Gothleplot left the vicarage to resume his trek to the Vermonts' property, unaware of their absence. They usually give him some food and let him sleep on an old blanket in the garage whenever he's passing through.

Jerry said, 'So when he realised the Vermonts weren't home he killed the ducks in frustration.'

According to Mr Gothleplot, he found the dead birds on the bank, appearing as though they'd been worried by a dog or a fox. Many feathers were scattered around, suggesting a third one had ben carried off. He thought the Vermonts may fancy a duck dinner, so he left them near the back door. Mr Gothleplot had slipped on his skin-tight glove before handling the corpses and didn't remove it, thus making his hand appear black in poor light ... or at least it would to someone who'd gone hours without sleep, believing the tramp was a dangerous man known as The Dark Hander.

Monika mentioned the gun she sometimes heard. By chance that very sound filled their ears before the officer could reply. PC Harrison explained this was Farmer Offalson's tactic to keep birds off his crops. Occasionally he has trouble with it going off after dark.

Jerry hoped Monika thought he looked as enlightened as she did upon hearing this revelation.

Following PC Harrison's departure, Jerry informed Monika that he too should go. She grabbed both his hands in hers, asking why he'd left that morning without saying anything.

'I woke up early and didn't want to disturb you. I left a note on the fridge, look.'

Monika waltzed over to read it, returning to her seat straight after with a beaming smile, grasping Jerry's hands again.

'I think you must really like me to write this.'

She leant forwards, giving him a peck on the lips. Jerry's voice was hoarse when he asked her to be his girlfriend. Monika nodded before moving onto his lap and giving him a kiss.

Jerry wandered home for some sleep an hour later. He'd arranged to have a quiet night out with Monika at The Upturned Table where Jerry would no longer care if the locals discussed women who talk to branches or the Demon of Grafton Field. And across the field Jerry sped that evening as the sun descended towards the horizon. He didn't mind the place in daylight hours when nothing eerie fermented the atmosphere.

He arrived at the Vermonts' house, hoping Monika would be ready, but alas! She'd decided to paint her nails and the drying time took longer than predicted. When she was ready, darkness prevailed. Once again Jerry had to hide the creepy feeling Grafton Field had over him when both solar and lunar lighting were absent.

'Oh look!' said Monika, pointing to their far right after climbing over the first stile. 'Mr Douglas has gone off the path to smell different cow mess tonight. Lucky I have you to walk me back later in case – ah! I forget! There is no Dark Hander! No more will I be scared of going down the Vermonts' track.'

As Jerry strained his eyes, just managing to discern the large figure on all fours in the distant blackness, he wished Monika didn't feel so brave in coming through this field with all its ghost stories. He'd much rather take the longer trek around the place.

They both froze when nearing the other end of the field: the man who'd just climbed over the stile was none other than Mr Douglass, ready for a stint of cowpat sniffing.

# A PROPOSAL

Dear Bathsheba

Although I walked out in a rage when you told me I'd impregnated you, try to understand how much of a shock this caused me. My aim now is to explain in writing that I've come to accept that my seed is growing inside of you and hope we can reunite. I've decided it makes sense for us to marry.

I bumped into your cousin Hamza half an hour ago. He said your family is wealthy enough to take care of you and the baby. Somehow, talking to him made me feel guilty for walking out on you. Despite your dishonesty, regarding your wealth – Hamza said you don't need to work, but desire independence – I forgive you.

Marriage is our way forward. Although I'm not rich, my pride won't be allowed to stand in the way of our happiness. Therefore, I'm happy to permit your family to pay for our union. In the meantime, let me convince you why I'm the only man worthy of your worship. Despite my being married and divorced, thus ruining your dreams of the perfect church wedding, no doubt your family's money will pay for Meckitt-Quick's registry office and for the fine rubber charcoal dress I've chosen for you. As it's short, skin-tight, and low-cut, we'll wait till after the birth, otherwise you'll be a bit of an eyesore. Ah yes, there're some black leather boots to go with it. Can't wait till all of my mates see me with you on my arm wearing this sexy outfit.

I've already arranged for the reception to be held at my favourite pub, The Bucket and Puke. Yes, you hate the place, but never mind. The landlord needs a cheque from your father to confirm the booking. I've made enquiries regarding the securing of a hotel room for a weekend honeymoon in Skegness.

Talking with Hamza gave me the impression that you're a little disappointed in me. He reckons you may not take me back! I laughed in his face when he told me this. Although this silly attitude surprises me, I don't fancy you any less for it. Afterwards I figured that any negativity was just your way of seeking attention. Thinking about it, you once mentioned something to me about not paying you enough attention – this is the verbal equivalent of foreplay in my book – so I've listed some romantic reminders of why we hooked up and should always stick together. If this doesn't clear away any doubts of marriage from your mind, I'll comb my hair with a hedgehog.

Remember the day we first met? To me it seems like yesterday. I think it was somewhere between January and May last year when you started work at the office. I could tell straight away that you fancied me. Most women do of course, though you seemed *really* into me. From my point of view, hardly a minute passed by without me wondering what you'd be like in the sack.

A couple of months later you couldn't stop smiling at me

during that work's night out. Several pints into the evening, I kept pinching your bum. What a firm arse you have, my dear – let's hope pregnancy doesn't add too much fat to it. Not long after this we had our first proper date when I took you to a pub quiz. You admitted how much you cared for me. I admitted how hot I thought you were.

Remember last September/October when you went into hospital to have your toe operated on? I couldn't stop thinking about you whilst sat alone in the pub with my friends. A week later I *had* to visit you in hospital. This shows my desire to be with you even when you're ill and we can't get frisky together.

Remember Halloween last year? Stupid question! You told me you loved me for the first time and I finally got to lay you – the first of many cracking moments between the sheets. Just think, if you were stupid enough to not want me for your husband, you'd never reach those dizzy heights of ecstasy again.

I knew it was more than just a physical thing between us when you bought me a laptop for Christmas while I got you that sexy lace underwear and a framed photo of me. That frame wasn't cheap, by the way. If these memories don't convince you that we should be united forever, think back to this Valentine's Day when you bought me a gold watch and modelled the thong I got you. What a night we had in that hotel room!

Of course, the downside came this Easter with the confirmation of my impregnation of you. I know now that walking out was a little rash, but with everything written here, I'm sure you can see how hard all this has been for me to cope with. Now that I've come to terms with this inconvenience, along with my acceptance of being poorer than you, there's nothing to keep us apart.

I'm working hard to ensure you won't have to be involved with the wedding at all until the day arrives. A taxi driver assures me that a Hackney cab will pick you up at five in the afternoon on whichever date we choose to marry. Note how I think of you by arranging the marriage so late in the day. This way you'll have plenty of time to recover from your hen night on the preceding evening. Although you've never tasted alcohol in your life – impressive, considering you're twenty-eight or twenty-nine – and have sworn not to, I presume you'll make an exception in this case. The cab driver also agreed to be a witness, at little extra cost to your family.

If, on the rare chance, any doubts surface about marrying me after reading this declaration of love, let me remind you that although we are both handsome individuals, when/if you do regain your now sublime figure after gaining weight through pregnancy, bear this in mind: not many guys will want to be lumbered with another man's mistake.

I'm expecting a positive response to this heartfelt marriage proposal.

Yours faithfully

Garth.

Dear Garth

Learning I was pregnant came as a big shock and I really needed your support. You hurt me by ignoring my calls and texts. Luckily Hamza and my parents have been by my side the whole time. Well, not the whole time. I still go to the bathroom on my own and my parents don't follow me to bed.

But Hamza does. Follow me to bed, that is; not watch me wee and you know what else. He's actually my *half* cousin. Even Dad thinks this doesn't count as incest and you know how particular he is regarding anything relating to the Ancient Egyptians. He still doesn't know about my secret picture of the Sphinx.

By the way, just because we've had sex forty-seven times doesn't mean I can't wear white to my wedding. If we did marry I'd pick my own dress and no way would I step foot in the Bucket and Puke after what happened last time with that lemon. And a Hackney cab? Really, Garth? You know they're always late and smell of strawberry air freshener. Can't you recall my allergies to all strawberry-scented thingummies?

I'm not going to respond to every detail in your message, as it would take ages, but those memories you noted of our time together did make me smile. Even so, I'm afraid you'll have to comb your hair with a hedgehog. When you walked out on me I saw another side of you that made me shudder like an I-don't-know-what.

I'll get Hamza to bring your hot water bottle back.

Love, Bathsheba.

# ALTERNATE ANGLES

## IAN

I rushed out of the airport toilets, over to my group of business associates. Theresa looked as hot as ever. She was also looking at *me* as much as ever; perhaps *more* than ever. Her eyes were drawn to my nether-regions when I got back from the gents'. No doubt she wanted to explore down there. I stood with the three guys from our group. Theresa sat next to Zoe, the only other female member of our entourage. I felt sure that when we landed in Paris there'd be an opportunity for me to get close to Theresa and make her day. I would've tried it on with her weeks ago, but she's one of those unapproachable types. Even though she's always staring at me whenever we're in the same room, her eyes – as beautiful as they are – have an intensity that puts me off. She never smiles at me either. Maybe Theresa's so into me that she's too shy to show any emotion. Perhaps she daren't risk the embarrassment of asking me out in case I turn her down. Rejection would be a big shock for a beauty like her. She needn't worry, though. I've fancied her since the day she started work at the office. Paris should be an ideal place to bring us together. Anyway, our plane's ready and waiting. I wonder if Theresa will sit next to Zoe on the flight or whether she'll feel confident enough to keep me company.

## THERESA

Whilst sat with four members of our group, the fifth one – Ian – came racing over to us from the airport toilet. What was he panicking for? I sat talking with Zoe, the only other lady in our group, while Ian joined the men. As usual he stood where he could see me. At times it's difficult not to stare at him. I've never met anyone so weird. I couldn't help noticing his fly was undone and shuddered at the thought of what lurked beneath his trousers. It's obvious he fancies me. Whenever we make eye contact at work his beady gaze gives me the creeps. He seems like the type who doesn't need much encouragement before you end up being unable to get rid of him. That's why whenever he says hello to me I don't smile when replying. He'd probably be stupid enough to interpret it as a come-on. Avoiding him in Paris will be difficult. I'd been really looking forward to this business trip – or rather the time-off from business – but once my boss announced that Ian was joining us it threw a wet blanket on the excursion. Still, Paris is a big place. Zoe and I will have to go off and do our own thing. Hopefully we'll meet some handsome Frenchmen. Anyway, our plane's ready for boarding. I'll have to stick close to Zoe now. There'll be no getting away from Ian if he sits beside me during the flight.

# STUNNED

As Emily drifted back towards consciousness her eyes flickered open and met with the patchy clouds moving overhead. The breeze against her bare arms and stomach added to her disorientation. Grogginess closed her eyes again, but memories of the morning began flowing back into her mind. She'd ignored her mother's advice about never stopping for hitchhikers no matter how innocent they appear.

The day began without any problems. Emily was a secretary at a legal firm in Hull. She didn't work Sundays, but with her boss unable to meet an important client in Lincoln, Emily deputised for him. As she'd grown up in this area before moving to Hull, she visited her parents in the nearby village of Kalesbury after the meeting.

Emily began the drive home at noon. The Lincolnshire back roads proved desolate on Sundays. As she turned a sharp corner the last thing she expected to see was a woman wearing a short dress and high heels, carrying only a handbag, walking along the grass bank.

The woman turned her head, hand raised, as Emily's BMW drew near. Although the day was mild for early March, the wind felt icy, making Emily sympathise for this young woman with bare arms and only nylons covering her legs. She hadn't forgotten her mother's advice about giving lifts to hitchhikers, but this was a beautiful woman dressed in a sexy outfit, miles from the nearest village. What if the next vehicle to come along was driven by a potential rapist or a murderer?

'Sorry, Mother,' said Emily under her breath, flicking the indicator on, 'but there are exceptions to every rule.'

The hiker rushed over to the car. She thanked Emily in an Eastern European accent, making herself comfortable in the passenger seat. For a moment there was a mutual feeling of surprise when they saw a resemblance of themselves in each other. Both women boasted high cheekbones, a pert nose, full lips, long dark-brown hair, and a slender figure. The only big difference was their eyes. Emily's were brown; her passenger's were blue and Slavic.

Driving on, Emily said, 'Where are you heading?'

'I must go to York but anywhere is fine so long as I am gone from Lincolnshire.'

When the woman crossed her legs Emily noticed a ladder in her tights, running the full length of her calf, and her shoes were muddy. Her beige dress also featured mud-stains splattered down the side.

'I'm going to Hull. I'm Emily, by the way.'

'I am Natalia. I will get a bus from the station.' She eyed Emily's skirt suit. 'You are on business?'

'I was. I'm heading home now.'

After a short while Emily's curiosity got the better of her. She asked Natalia why she was wandering alone in the middle of nowhere.

'I had a bad date.' She pointed at Emily's gold chain. 'I like your necklace.'

'Me too.' She touched the heart in the centre. 'My boyfriend bought me it.'

'He must – why you stop?'

Emily stepped on the brake before parking near the grass bank. She reached for her handbag on the back seat and rummaged through it.

'Damn! Thought so! I've left my phone at my parents' house.'

She made a three-point turn and headed back.

After a minute's silence Emily said, 'I don't have a watch. Do –'

'Is nearly two o'clock,' said Natalia, raising her left wrist.

'Nearly two – well, I know me turning back is annoying, but it's better than –'

'Is fine.' Natalia ran her fingers through her dark tresses. 'I have a cousin in Hull. Maybe you are near each other?'

'I live down Scarleton Street –'

'Scar-ler-ton Street! This where my cousin stay. What number you live?'

'17. Why –'

'Ah! He live at Number 2. You probably not seen him. You are renting?'

Emily nodded, saying, 'I hope to buy my own place next year; 2004 at the latest. Where are you from? What country, I mean?'

'Po-land.' Natalia interlocked her fingers and twiddled her thumbs. 'You are doing well for one so young. You are nineteen?'

'No, I am *not* nineteen. I'm twenty-two.'

'One year younger than me. Do – wait!' Natalia stared at the crossroads looming ahead. 'Which way is Kalesbury?'

'Left.'

Natalia clutched Emily's arm.

'You cannot go left! Stop the car!'

'What's the matter?'

Emily halted at the crossroads.

'Take me to Hull!' Natalia searched through her handbag. 'Come back later for your phone!'

'Are you in some sort of – what's that?'

Natalia held up an object four inches long, two inches wide, rectangular-shaped, black, with two silver circular attachments placed a couple of inches apart on the end pointing at Emily.

'This is a stun gun. It will knock you out for five minute. We drove by a track before. Go back there.'

'What's going on?'

Natalia thrust the weapon towards Emily's shoulder.

'Do it! Keep your hands on the wheel and do not drive more than 40.'

Emily gritted her teeth as she turned the car around at the crossroads. No more words were uttered until they approached the track several minutes later.

'Stop here! Turn!'

Emily didn't exceed 5 mph along the bumpy lane.

'17 Scar-ler-ton Street is your home?'

'Yes. Why –'

'Keep looking at the track! Is meant for tractors. I do not want to be stuck.'

Emily drove on until they reached a hedge. A muddy field lay to their right. Another hedge separated them from the field on their left. As Emily switched off the ignition, Natalia jabbed the stun gun against her shoulder.

Natalia shot out of the car and rushed over to the driver's side. She scooped Emily up off the seat, carried her a few paces from the vehicle, and dumped her on the ground. She stripped Emily down to her underwear and tights before removing her own dress and high heels. With both women being of medium height and possessing a toned figure, Emily's clothes and shoes were a perfect fit for Natalia.

The heaviness eased from Emily's eyelids. Again her vision landed on the clouds swimming above. She remembered everything now. Waking up attired in just her underwear and nylons caused a new panic. She attempted to rise, but grogginess held her down. A second effort found her sat with legs curled to one side, hands palms down on the ground. Her blazing eyes focused on Natalia buttoning up her 'new' suit jacket.

'What the *hell* are you doing!'

Natalia reached inside the car for the beige dress and muddy shoes.

'I must go. I cannot be recognised – Here!'

The shoes fell near Emily's knees as she knelt upright. The garment landed on the muddy field.

'Why didn't you lie on the back seat if you wanted to keep out of sight?'

'I will not risk anything. We look very much the same, so when you walk to Kalesbury, hide if you see a silver Metro.'

'Why, for goodness' sake!'

She rose to her feet. Natalia pointed the stun gun at her.

'I will have your necklace.'

Emily made a grab for the stun gun. Natalia dodged out of the way. Emily staggered to one side after stepping on a large stone. Natalia edged closer, thrust the stun gun against Emily's waist, dropping her like a bag of cement. She swiped the necklace, jumped into the car, and drove away.

When Emily's eyes opened after being rendered unconscious for a second time they rested on the muddy field. Several minutes later she shook off the loose dirt from the beige dress. A mud-stain resembling a map of Japan decorated the front of the expensive garment. Emily slipped it on, grimacing as the damp material clung to her waist. She carried the dirty shoes with her down the bumpy lane. The sole of her left foot tingled from landing on the stone.

She recalled Natalia's warning about avoiding a silver

Metro. Could Emily trust anything she'd said? Why would that selfish woman do her any favours? Yet on the other hand why did Natalia leave the dress and shoes when she could've kept them?

She slid on the three-inch heels after reaching the end of the track. The chances of finding help on the back roads during a quiet Sunday were minimal. Emily's fury rose, thinking about how she'd stopped to give a lift to someone appearing vulnerable, yet all the thanks she received was to be put in that same uncertain predicament.

Emily needed to commence the long trek to Kalesbury. Her phone and spare keys were at her parents' house. Anyway, why let Natalia ruin her day any more than she had already? That woman could not be trusted. If Emily saw a Metro she'd flag it down.


The first ten minutes of walking was endurable but when the flat road became a steep hill Emily's heels and nylons proved to be more unsuitable hiking footwear than previously.

With the hill conquered fifteen minutes later, a more even surface stretched out before her. Emily rested on the bank, massaging her aching feet. This respite was brief. The strong March wind blew colder, bringing goosebumps to her bare arms. She gave them a rub before recommencing her trek.

She'd driven over these quiet roads many times yet never took in the enormity of the surroundings. Green fields spread out for miles at either side with trees bordering them on the horizon. Her situation prevented the scenic view from being enjoyable. An hour had elapsed since she'd been abandoned. The darkening clouds zoomed faster overhead as Emily neared the last crossroads before Kalesbury.

A left turn and five minutes later a car appeared in the distance. Although it was travelling the opposite way she hoped the driver would stop and let her use their mobile to call her parents. She stood statuesque as a black Fiat Panda halted near the bank. A blonde woman, twenty years Emily's senior and three stones heavier, sat behind the steering wheel. She wound the window down.

'Get in.'

Emily thought the woman sounded like she was making a demand, not an offer. Her face was like a stone gargoyle's.

'I'm going the opposite way; to Kalesbury.'

The woman's hard countenance altered to a more sly expression.

'I'll take you. It's not safe for a young lass to be wandering alone on these roads.'

Emily hesitated, finding the woman intimidating. She glanced overhead at the dark sky. The wind blew colder against her arms, swirling around her legs. If a storm was coming she didn't want to be caught in it. This woman appeared menacing, though what were the chances of meeting another Natalia in the same day? The likelihood wasn't as great as that of the threatening clouds.

She settled into the passenger seat, introducing her name. The driver was called Violet. When they set off the opposite way Emily didn't ask her why she didn't make a three-point turn and head for Kalesbury as she assumed she'd turn at the crossroads.

'That's a pretty dress you've got on, Em'ly.'

'Thanks, but it's not mine.'

'You don't say. Found it, eh?'

'No, it's a long – the crossroads are coming up if you want to turn round.'

'I need to do something at 'ome first.'

Emily eased one leg over the other and removed her shoe. She sighed, massaging the stone imprint in her tender sole.

'Been doing too much running about the countryside, eh?'

'Too much walking.'

'You've got good legs on you but you're wearing the wrong type of shoes. I 'ad a figure like yours once. I climbed a few dress sizes after me 'usband died. With ma daughter just turning eighteen I sorted out the best of me old outfits to give 'er this morning. I can see 'em fitting you perfectly too.'

Emily nodded in response, gazing outside, stewing about what Natalia had done. She was only half-listening until a long fingernail prodded her thigh.

She shot Violet a stern glance.

'I'd a dress just like what you're wearing.'

Violet pinched at the short hemline, nipping Emily in the process.

'Do you mind!'

Emily rubbed her leg.

'Ma dress was exactly the same as yours.'

'Really!' She sighed, shaking her head. 'Like I said, this isn't mine.'

'Aye, so you said. You've got it shitted up, though. Fell over?'

'No, it was – what's that smell outside? Something's burning.'

Emily spied a smouldering field.

'Firemen stopped it before it reached me 'ouse,' said Violet, pointing at a bungalow near the roadside.

She drove into a small front yard. Emily glanced at the building as they parked, thinking it looked like a well-kept place, yet found it odd that all the curtains were closed.

'Shall I wait for you?'

'Nah. Come in. This won't take long, but too long for you to sit alone in ma car. Wouldn't want you 'ot-wiring it and buggering off now, would we?'

Emily smiled, replacing her shoe, though suspected Violet wasn't joking.

They exited the Fiat and strolled towards the front

door.

'How did the fire start?'

Violet's face and tone of voice were hard when she replied.

'Ma son set it ablaze.'

The women stared at each other until Violet broke eye-contact to unlock the door.

'Is your son okay? Where is he?'

''Ee's spending the night in 'ospital. It shocked 'im.'

Emily, feeling relieved that the fire-starting son wasn't home, entered the bungalow. Violet flicked the light and kettle on in the kitchen. She left the curtains drawn.

'Tea?'

'Water, please. Could I use your phone to –'

'We don't 'ave a landline. You can borrow ma mobile after I've sent a text.'

Emily leaned against the kitchen worktop while Violet typed out a message.

'Shit! That text used up the last of ma credit. I'll drive you to Kalesbury after I've 'ad a drink.'

The women headed to the medium-sized living room. Violet switched the light on, rather than opening the curtains, like she'd done in the kitchen. The carpet appeared worn and the wallpaper was peeling here and there. They sat opposite each other in red armchairs that matched each other but not the leather couch.

Emily took a drink before placing her glass of water on a small table beside her chair.

'How old is your son?' she said, clasping her hands around her knee.

'Ricky's seventeen, but only in years.'

'I don't understand.'

''Ee 'as some problems up 'ere.' She tapped her head. ''Ee's not a nut-job, but 'ee's easily mislead, like 'ee was in burning that bloody field.' She glared at Emily. 'What do you make of a bitch 'oo takes advantage of a young lad 'oo isn't quite right upstairs?'

Natalia's face popped into Emily's mind. She understood Violet's accusing glare.

'Did he meet someone resembling me? Because –'

'Resembling you, my arse!' Violet rose from her chair. ''Ow you've the nerve to come back 'ere, thinking Ricky was too daft to say ought –'

'You're confusing me with –'

'It's took all ma bloody patience to keep calm this long and not break your nose!'

'Now just you damn well listen!' Emily shot to her feet, standing face to face with Violet. 'I'm – get *off* me!'

The heavier woman seized Emily's slender wrist and twisted it up behind her back. She gripped Emily's free arm above the elbow with her other hand. She marched her forwards through an open door leading to the bedrooms.

Emily's attempts to break free were quashed by increased pressure to her arm. All protests were ignored as they rushed towards the master bedroom door, currently ajar. Emily cried out as she collided into it, forcing it wide open. She screeched again when Violet sent her hurtling into the foot of the double bed. She turned, off-balance, receiving a punch in the stomach, dropping her to her knees.

Violet flicked on the light before holding up a suitcase lying on the bed, speaking as though nothing serious just happened.

'Remember this?'

Emily looked up, gasping.

'It was near that 'edge between the burning field and the next one.' Violet opened the case. 'I was gonna give these to ma daughter Jane.' She held up a satin dress. 'Me 'usband liked me to wear sexy things when I 'ad a good figure. Since 'ee died I lost interest in dieting and whatnot. I decided to save ma best dresses for Jane when she turned eighteen.'

'Listen –'

'Imagine 'ow pissed off I was coming 'ome to find the field at the back of the 'ouse ablaze, ma son shitting 'imself, and when fire brigade 'ad buggered off, think 'ow I felt walking in 'ere seeing these were missing.'

Emily remained kneeling, her pain easing, listening to Violet recall how her son described meeting a beautiful brunette in Lincoln. He was sat on a bench when she approached him, introducing herself as Natalie. She explained that if she didn't raise enough money her baby – residing in York Hospital – would die. She persuaded Ricky to help her.

Emily interrupted: 'Her name's *Natalia*. She's Po –'

'*You* told Ricky to keep everything secret and made sure this place was empty before getting a bus 'ere.'

'Surely he told you Natalia had blue eyes and a foreign accent?'

''Ee wouldn't notice what colour a lass's eyes were! 'Ee just told me you was a stunner and didn't talk like us. Posh is same as foreign.'

'I'm not posh!'

Violet raised her leg and slammed the sole of her foot against Emily's chest, forcing her onto her back. She missed cracking her head against the bedroom wall by an inch.

'Ricky said you'd told 'im that nobody'd dare 'elp you cos the frigging FBI were chasing you! You told 'im if 'ee married you the government'd pay a doctor to save your baby's life.'

Emily rolled onto her side.

'It wasn't me who – Ugh!'

A kick in the thighs silenced her.

'Bitch! Taking *my* money to piss off to bloody York! What were you gonna do with the clothes I left out? Sell 'em?'

Emily lay quiet on her side, glancing at the open door whenever Violet looked away. She needed to be off the floor with some distance between the two of them before making a run for it. She was much fitter than the older woman, though not only had she been assaulted, Violet wore trainers, offering a great advantage over high heels. She thought about kicking her shoes off, but if she raced outside and cut her foot open, she'd probably get dragged back indoors by the hair. For now she must stay patient.

'No doubt you told Ricky to charge out the back way with you when me and Jane pulled up outside. 'Ee said you shit yourself when you 'eard us. 'Ee thought we wouldn't be back for ages and told you as much. Bet that's why you were trying on me old dress, thinking there was time to spare. Cheeky bitch! Not 'appy with nicking ma stuff you 'ad to try ma bloody clothes on while you were invading the bastard 'ouse!'

Emily curled into a ball, covering her head, as Violet's temper erupted again.

'You must've left ma suitcase near the field bottom ready for when we went out again. You don't take from *me!* Get that bastard thing off and wash it!'

Violet grabbed Emily's calves and yanked her legs away from her body. She went down on one knee, delivering a hard punch to her stomach. In her battered state there was nothing Emily could do to stop Violet from wrenching the garment off her body.

'At least you're not wearing ma fucking underwear! The tights aren't mine; I don't wear natural, but do those bastard shoes belong to me?'

'I d-don't know! Natalia left – Ugh!'

Another kick in the thighs.

'Don't take me for a silly bitch! You can keep 'em on for now at least, but this dress is for ma daughter. You can wash it in a minute.' Violet dropped the garment on the floor, inches away from Emily. 'I've told Ricky before to stop messing about with bits of flint cos 'ee'd end up burning something 'ee shouldn't. 'Ee was showing off to impress *you*, and you left 'im when the fire spread, not even checking if 'ee was okay. I saw you when me and Jane came outside.'

Violet walked past the bed, over to a built-in wardrobe.

Emily's large bosom still quickened, though the pain in her stomach had eased enough to speak without gasping.

'Natalia's Polish. Obviously she needs to get married to stay in this country.'

Violet marched back, scooped up the beige dress, and threw it in Emily's face.

'I saw you with my own bloody eyes, wearing *that* dress, you conning slut! You shot through that fucking 'edge like a fox with its arse ablaze!'

'Please!' Emily raised her hands. 'Hear me out! I can explain everything.'

Violet loomed over her, listening to how she'd stopped to give a beautiful Polish woman a lift, only to be left stunned, stripped, and stranded.

'If you phone the police and report my car as stolen they might catch Natalia.'

'Thing is,' said Violet, walking back to her wardrobe, 'I don't 'ave faith in cops.' She opened the wardrobe. 'Me 'usband was stabbed by an intruder – I was caught unawares and bashed over the 'ead, otherwise I would've killed the fucker.' She knelt down as Emily sat upright against the wall. ''Ee died trying to protect our 'ouse – our old 'ouse, not this one.' She rummaged around the bottom of the wardrobe. 'The cops never found the bastard that did it. Luckily Ricky and Jane weren't touched.'

'I'm sorry,' said Emily, kneeling upright, 'but now you know I'm –'

'I don't believe a bloody word of it.'

Violet stood up, clutching a rounders' bat.

Emily was back on her feet. Her stomach tightened as fear spread through her body. Was this enraged woman going to beat her to death?

'Th-there are people you can call who'll prove –'

'I don't believe ought that spouts from that arsehole in your face. As if two lasses looking the same'd meet by chance and swap clothes!'

'As a decoy!' Emily backed away. 'A decoy that's –'

'Stay still!' Violet raised the bat. 'Pick that frigging dress up!'

Emily maintained eye contact as she crouched down for the garment.

'Natalia asked me which street I live down. She must've wanted to lie low for a while. If you took me to Hull –'

'There could be a den of conning bastards in 'Ull!'

'If –'

'Shut your bloody arsehole! I texted Jane earlier, telling 'er to stop driving around cos I'd got you. We're gonna 'ave *our* justice.'

'What do mean? What are you going to do?'

'What's up? Feeling scared? Can't be any more scary than it was for ma Ricky being left stranded by a lass 'ee thought liked 'im, thinking she'd left 'im to burn to death.'

'Listen to –'

'Shut your hole and get to the bastard kitchen!'

Violet kept prodding Emily with the bat on their short journey through the bungalow.

As they entered the kitchen Emily watched Violet lock up before hanging the keys on a copper hook near the front door. Her mind raced for an idea of escape. To grab the keys and run now would be futile with Violet stood nearby holding the rounders' bat.

'Fill that sink with water. You can scrub that dress clean if it takes all afternoon.'

'Can I have some clothes to wear?'

'What's the problem? Feeling vulnerable? Ricky's a vulnerable lad and you took advantage of that. Anyway, if you 'adn't nabbed what's mine you'd still be wearing your own kit.' Violet took a box of washing powder from a cupboard near Emily's leg and slammed it on the draining board. 'Mix in plenty of this.'

Emily lifted the box, scanning everything around the sink area. Could something be used as a weapon against this violent woman? The small sponge and dishcloth weren't going to help. Perhaps the can of air freshener might come in handy though. Whilst tipping powder into the water she speculated what Violet's 'justice' entailed. She'd already been beaten up. Was that the worst of it? Was she enduring the rest of her 'punishment' now? Did Violet just want her to feel scared and susceptible by having to wash a dress whilst attired in her underwear and nylons with the constant threat of being attacked? Perhaps Violet wanted her daughter to view Emily in her current sorry state before letting her go.

She noticed the absence of Marigolds on the draining board. If Violet looked away to get some from a cupboard that might be the best chance of escape. Although she ached from being assaulted her adrenalin was now pumped up. Emily felt ready to get out of there and, if possible, take the dress before getting it wet. Earlier she'd wished for more practical attire, yet now this would be like a warm jumper compared to the alternative.

'Could I have some gloves, please?'

'Why would I do *you* any favours?'

'Please. My hands come out in a rash if I don't use gloves.'

'I don't give a shit if they come out in grape-sized warts with bright-yellow puss oozing out of 'em!'

'Okay, okay!'

Emily raised her hands as Violet stepped forward.

'Now get the bloody thing washed or else I'll dunk your bastard face in the sink!'

Emily was an intelligent woman. She needed to think of something in a matter of seconds to escape safe and clothed. In the end, with such little resources at hand, she tried an old-school bluff.

Emily grasped the dress in one hand, appearing like

she was about to drop it in the sink. At the last moment she widened her eyes, parting her lips, glancing over Violet's shoulder. Before doing this Emily knew the two possible outcomes. Violet would either ask what she was staring at without checking to see for herself or she'd be curious enough to investigate. This was a huge risk. Violet should know nothing was amiss in her own house. On the other hand she was an untrusting woman.

'What the hell are you gawking at?' Violet turned her head. 'You dozy – Argh!'

Emily had grabbed the can of air freshener the moment those menacing eyes left her. She sprayed it into Violet's face when she turned back round.

Violet dropped the bat and brought both hands to her stinging eyes.

Emily slung the dress over one shoulder after claiming the fallen weapon. She swung it at the back of Violet's head, sending her flying forwards, crashing face-first on the ground. Emily snatched the keys from their copper hook. In her desperation to unlock the front door she dropped the bat, hoping the first of five keys on the ring would offer freedom. When it failed she glanced at Violet, still swearing, though her eyes were recovering. Emily opened the door on her third attempt.

She raced from the house, sprinted to the Fiat, jumped behind the steering wheel, and started the engine. She glanced at the bungalow. Violet staggered through the doorway, rubbing her sore eyes. Emily zoomed out of the yard, almost colliding with a silver Metro.

Emily drove for ten minutes before pulling into a layby. In haste she slipped on the dress before continuing the drive to Kalesbury. A torrent of emotions swirled round in her mind. If only she hadn't stopped for Natalia this nightmare wouldn't be happening. She'd never wanted to see her mother and father so much as she did now. She repressed her tears whilst driving, but they started leaking out after parking outside her parents' home.

The absence of her father's car was a concern. If he'd gone out on a Sunday, chances were his wife would've accompanied him. The confirmation came when nobody answered the door.

Emily took her mother's spare back door key from under a big plant pot in the garden. She let herself in and raced to the living room. Her mobile was not apparent. She searched the kitchen. Nothing. Almost hyperventilating, feeling dizzy, she sat on a wooden chair at the kitchen table, attempting to compose herself. Her father once said, if you can't find something you've lost, you'll probably see it after giving up the search. This almost applied when Emily's gaze rested on the fridge door, sighting a note written by her mother.

The message read:

*Dear Emily, if you're reading this you must've come back for your phone. I saw it after waving goodbye. We waited an hour to see if you'd return. When you didn't, I thought we should bring it to Hull, knowing you need it for work. With us visiting friends in Newark later I'll post it through the letterbox. Your father's put it inside one of those bubble envelopes. Hope this hasn't spoiled your day too much. Love you, darling. Mother xxx*

Reading this affectionate note brought tears to her eyes. Just a simple message, filled with parental love. How would her mother feel if she knew how her beloved daughter had been treated? Emily felt desperate to speak to her parents yet couldn't remember their mobile numbers. She searched the phone book on the table, hoping they'd written them down, but no. They hadn't noted their daughter's number either. Storing it on their mobiles proved sufficient.

However, Emily *could* ring the police. She should've done this first, but all she could think of was the comfort her parents would give. No one had ever broken her spirit before or even hit her till today. She needed to regain composure and make the call. Violet and Natalia should not be allowed to get away with their crimes.

Emily remained seated in the kitchen beside the landline phone on the table. She dialled 999. Having spoken three words to the person on the other end, the line went dead. She slammed the receiver down and tried again. Emily placed the phone to her ear: no dial tone. She wanted to scream, but no; she needed to stay focused.

Emily grabbed her spare house keys from the little box on the wall, thinking how her mother's advice to cut a spare set for them to look after had proved to be a blessing. She hurried out the back way, returning her parents' door key under the plant pot. She opened the garden gate and stepped onto the drive, meeting with more bad luck.

'I don't believe this!'

She couldn't reverse the Fiat down the drive now that a silver Metro blocked the way. As both front doors opened, Emily dropped her keys, recognising the passenger.

Violet, wearing an unzipped long coat, stood beside her eighteen-year-old daughter.

'Jane got back as you were buggering off. Spotting ma car didn't take long in this tiny piss'ole of a village. 'Ope you didn't mind me cutting the phone line. Thought you might be spending time talking and I ain't got time to waste. I was about to send Jane to knock on the door. Glad you decided to come out and see us.'

Emily crouched down for her keys, but Violet's foot landed on top of them.

'If you try anything the neighbours –'

'You've pinched ma bloody car for fuck's sake!'

'Only because –'

'I'll drop the charges if you 'elp us.'

'Help *you*!'

'The police phoned ten minutes ago. They've

matched the description of the lass Ricky told 'em about. Copper said a Polish lass's visa ran out and she's disappeared. If she can find some poor sod to marry 'er she can stay in the country. You were telling the truth after all.'

'Yes, and if you'd just listened –'

'So you reckon the bitch 'as pissed off to 'Ull, eh?'

'I can't think why else she wanted my address, but –'

'Either I call the cops and report you for nicking ma car or we go to your 'ouse.' Violet scooped up the keys. 'Jane can gimme an alibi if you're thinking of speaking up about what *didn't* 'appen earlier. I could show the cops the massive bump on the back of me skull and say you whacked me before pinching ma car. Seeing as I made a cock up by thinking you was the bitch we wanted, I'll forget about you attacking me if you play ball. It's this Natalie, Natalia, or whatever she's called that we want. Are you gonna lead us to your 'ouse or not?'

Emily hung her head, guessing the police would believe the mother of a teenage boy with learning difficulties, backed up by her daughter. She could be charged for car theft and perhaps be held in detention until someone could vouch for her identity. Even if Emily could prove her bruises had been attained from being assaulted, Violet could claim she was defending herself and the Fiat from being stolen. Emily would lose her job if her boss found out. The chances of finding another high-paid position in a legal firm would be unlikely.

She had to submit to Violet's demands. At least with the truth now known, Violet's 'justice' would be exacted on Natalia. Emily despised the Polish woman for abandoning her, but felt she should be reported to the police, not surrendered to this vigilante. That said, she wasn't doing any favours for Natalia, who may not have gone to her house anyway. Even if she had, she could've long since departed. Emily thought that if Violet accompanied her to Hull at least she'd be home. Her boyfriend was due to visit her today. If she was lucky they may get there when he calls round.

'I've no choice!' Emily massaged her forehead. 'I'm travelling alone, though. You can follow me.'

'And give us the slip? No chance! Jane'll take the Metro and follow us in the Fiat. I'll look after your 'ouse keys. Let's go.'


Both women remained mute after leaving Kalesbury. Emily spoke up when spotting the turn-off leading to Hull.

'Slow down! You'll miss the – what are you doing? You've driven past –'

'I'm not wasting petrol by using both cars. We're leaving this one and taking the Metro.'

With the truth about Natalia revealed, Emily hadn't felt too uneasy about being back in Violet's presence, but the thought of returning to *that* bungalow rekindled her fear.

When they arrived Violet waited for Jane to exit the Metro before she and Emily got out of the Fiat.

Emily felt the increasing wind chill and specks of rain hit her as she stood near Jane's car. She forgot about the weather when Violet slapped her face.

'That's for nicking ma bloody car and making me chase you to frigging Kalesbury!'

Emily stood open-mouthed, pressing a hand to her smarting cheek.

'Get in the back!'

She didn't need telling twice. As she ducked inside, a pounding blow thundered against her lower back.

'That's for cracking ma fucking 'ed!'

Violet shoved Emily with both hands, sending her sprawling forwards. She landed face-down on the car floor. Violet clambered along the seat and grabbed a tuft of Emily's hair and clutched her upper arm. Jane seized Emily's calves. Mother and daughter hauled her off the floor, onto the seat, and spun her over. Violet, sitting sideways-on behind the driver's seat, held her in a headlock, clasping her left wrist. Jane gripped the other wrist and sat on Emily's legs.

'Take this as a warning. If you try ought daft between 'ere and 'Ull we'll tear you to pieces. You're gonna show us where you live and take us inside like we're all good friends. If that bitch is there we'll take 'er away with us. If she's not we'll leave as though nought's 'appened. Cross me just once; make a fuss, do ought to make folk ask questions, and I'll do a lot more than spray bastard air freshener into your bloody eyes. Got it?'

Violet manhandled Emily into a sitting-upright position behind the passenger seat. She bound her wrists together with the middle seatbelt and buckled her in with the passenger belt, leaving her hands static on her lap.

'That'll stop you waving at anyone we pass on our way.'

Jane climbed into the driver's seat. Violet sat behind her with the rounders' bat across her lap and a fold-out knife in her hand.

Emily could still feel Violet's choking arm and the seatbelt dug into her wrists as they began the journey from Lincolnshire to Hull. She could only hope that Violet would let her go as promised. She'd only treated her like this through not trusting her and, being a vengeful person, was also repaying her for fighting back and stealing the car. Emily clung to the belief that once she was home this nightmare would end. Violet would eventually face the consequences of her actions, though right now that was a small comfort.

Time passed by. The Humber Bridge came into view. Violet shuffled over to the middle seat. She gripped Emily's chin.

'Don't make a sound when Jane opens the window to pay the bridge toll, unless you want a knife in your guts.'

Several minutes later they joined a short queue at one

of the ticket booths. Violet clasped a hand on Emily's bare shoulder whilst positioning the other – holding the knife – on the captive's lap.

As Jane opened the window, Emily felt almost too nervous to breathe, sensing the knife point touching her stomach. Violet removed the weapon when Jane drove on, though grasped Emily's upper arm, resting her knife hand on Emily's leg.

'This is where you start giving us directions.'

Emily felt sickened by Violet's touch and petrified of the knife hovering so close to her body. One bump in the road may cause an inch or two of cold steel to delve into her thigh.

She felt closer to home yet by returning she felt nearer to danger. She thought of how Violet may erupt if Natalia wasn't present. Emily could get beaten up instead, worse than before. Perhaps she'd get stabbed too. Natalia wanting her address didn't guarantee she'd go there. She'd been determined to reach York. Perhaps she'd been to rob Emily just as she'd intended to steal from Violet. If so, she would've been and gone. Emily thought that Natalia may have stopped elsewhere first, assuming she had time to spare, knowing Emily's chances of getting a lift on those deserted back roads would be difficult.

They drove down Scarleton Street after five o'clock. Emily saw her car parked nearby. She told Violet this, proving that Natalia had been here, though did she abandon the BMW and go?

Jane parked the Metro beside the alley leading to the back of Emily's house. Violet gave the knife to her daughter before slotting the rounders' bat into a holder inside her coat.

She clamped a hand on Emily's leg, digging her fingernails in as she spoke: 'We're gonna get out soon and walk to your 'ouse. Don't try getting your neighbours' attention, or scream, or try running off, or else I'll break your bloody fingers. Play ball and you soon won't 'ave to see us again.'

Violet exited the car. Jane clambered from the front of the vehicle onto the middle seat, pressing the flat of the knife against Emily's waist. Violet opened the rear passenger door. She reached in, unbuckled her captive's seatbelt, and untied her hands.

Emily gasped in relief, clutching her numb fingers. Red marks indented her wrists.

'Stay put, Jane, and remember what to do.'

Violet grabbed Emily's forearm and dragged her from the car. She seized her hand, interlocking their fingers like they were lovers.

Black clouds made it darker than usual for the time of day. Emily blinked as drizzle blew into her face as they passed three houses before stopping at Number 17. With hindsight she thought her best option would've been not agreeing to this crazy idea. Being charged for car theft and losing her job no longer seemed so bad. But it was too late. Any hope of a neighbour popping outside was unlikely on a dank Sunday in March.

Violet clutched Emily's hand as she unlocked the front door. She opened and closed it without making a noise. They stood in a small hallway near the foot of the stairs. Two of Emily's suitcases were apparent, presumably filled with her belongings, implying that Natalia was still here.

Violet unlocked her fingers from Emily's.

'Take *my* dress off.'

'Why – Mmmph!'

Violet slapped a palm over Emily's mouth, slamming her head against the wall near the bottom of the stairs. With her other hand clasping her throat, she spoke in a whisper.

'That dress is for Jane. The bitch 'oo left ma Ricky for dead is gonna wash it. You can change into your own clothes soon. I don't know why you're fussing. Now strip!'

Emily let out a huge sigh as the unwelcome hands

removed themselves from her throat and mouth. The menacing look in Violet's eye was the only prompt she needed to remove the garment. This was the third time in one afternoon she had to face somebody in her underwear and tights. At least this time she wasn't being unclothed by another woman.

Once stripped, Violet snatched the dress, stepped behind her, twisted the garment, and wrapped it round Emily's neck like a noose. She held it in place with one hand and clamped her other palm over Emily's mouth, warning her to do exactly as demanded, unless she wanted throttling.

Of everything Emily had endured today nothing scared her more than this moment in her own home. She didn't doubt Violet would wring her neck. She was almost choking her now.

One of the main reasons Emily stopped to give Natalia a lift was the sight of her wearing a short dress and high heels, believing that a beautiful woman walking alone attired in a sexy outfit was prone to dangerous men. The same dress alerting Emily's concern for another's safety may now cause her own death at the hands of a dangerous woman.

They shuffled forwards.

'Open that door! Slowly.'

Emily couldn't see the handle with her head forced back, though knowing her own house she found and turned it. The door opened a crack.

'Give it a big shove!'

Emily used what little power she could muster in her restricted position and slammed her palms against the door. Violet stayed still until it swung wide open. They entered the living room, stepping sideways. Violet eased the door shut with her foot.

A cup, a plate, a knife and fork sat on the coffee table. A bubble envelope lay ripped open on the couch. The mobile phone it once contained now resided in

Natalia's handbag. The toilet flushed. The kitchen separated the bathroom from the living room. They stood listening for more sounds of life. Emily's restricted breathing quickened as the clacking of high heels became audible on the kitchen floor.

The door opened.

Natalia entered the room wearing Emily's skirt and blouse, along with an un-laddered pair of her tights. She froze; stunned by the apparition in the living room.

Violet shoved Emily forwards, sending her crashing over an armchair, onto a small ottoman storage box. She flung the beige dress over one shoulder before producing the rounders' bat from under her coat. She shot forward, kicked the kitchen door shut, and stood with her back to it.

Natalia began to run, only to be thrown off balance by the impact of the bat whacking against her shoulder. A second strike to the back of her knees floored her. She attempted to rise. Violet booted Natalia in the stomach and dragged her upright by the hair. She cried out, trying to dislodge the hand tugging at her dark locks. Another punch to the stomach silenced her.

Violet shoved Natalia onto the couch. She turned, finding Emily back on her feet. She kneed her in the thigh and pushed her backwards into the armchair opposite the couch.

Violet hovered between the two distressed women, raising the bat. Her stony gaze rested on Natalia.

'In case you're wondering what the hell's going on, I'm the mother of that young lad you left to burn in a field today.'

'I do not know what you talk about!'

'Don't take me for an idiot, bitch! The cops told me about a Polish lass 'oose visa ran out. This slut told me you'd be 'ere.'

Natalia's beautiful yet severe Slavic eyes glanced at Emily before meeting Violet's menacing glare.

'Okay, but it was not me who did burn that field. It was –'

'Ricky; I know, but 'ee don't know any better. Blame 'im again an' I'll whack this bat so 'ard into your face you'll look like you've got a second arse ... So what would you 'ave done with ma son if you'd both gone to York?'

'I would have married him. I do not want to go back to Po-land. I cannot go back.'

'You would've married 'im, eh? Then what? Lived together 'appily ever after?'

'Yes, I would have lived with him. Even though he is retarded –'

'Retarded!' Violet raised the bat with her voice. 'I'll give you retarded, you fucking whore! 'Ee 'as problems but – what *you* doing, bitch!'

Violet spun round, hearing Emily lift the ottoman storage box lid beside her chair.

One distraction led to another. Natalia leapt up, grabbing the knife from the coffee table. She ran past the couch to the opposite side of the room, halting near a cabinet where she'd left the stun gun.

Violet strode towards her.

'Get back on – what the hell's that?'

'Is stun gun! Keep back or you will feel it!'

Natalia held it up in her right hand, brandishing the knife in her left.

Violet stepped back, remembering Emily's story.

During the confrontation Emily snatched her metal dumbbells from the ottoman. They measured fourteen inches long and with one in each hand she'd armed herself with a pair of formidable weapons. For the first time since her ordeal began it felt like she was taking back some control.

The three women stood like the points of a triangle, glancing at one another in turn, each with their weapons half raised.

Glancing from Emily to Natalia, and finally referring

to herself, Violet said, 'This is like the slut, the bad, and the righteous.'

Emily, referring to herself before glancing at Violet and Natalia in turn, said, 'It's more like the abused, the mad, and the dodgy.'

Natalia narrowed her eyes, shaking her head.

'I do not know what the hell you both say, but Emily, we have the common enemy. We should rush her.'

'Yes, and during the ruckus I'll get jabbed with that damn thing again! As if I'd trust a word you say after what you did to me.'

'Let me tell you bitches something: I told Jane to come in through the front door if I'm not back after ten minutes.'

Natalia huffed, saying, 'I do not believe. Why not ring now if this is true?'

'Cos I want both 'ands on me bat, you conning slapper! Anyway, your friend'll tell you I'm not bullshitting, won't you, eh?'

'Her daughter is out there.' Emily shifted her gaze from Natalia to Violet, saying, 'That woman is no friend of mine. I hope you're going to keep your word and –'

'Do you know what I've thought since the cops phoned? I reckon you two were partners. A pair of scamming bitches. Today you 'ad a disagreement, probably to do with our foreign friend 'ere 'aving visa troubles. Whatever it was that's why you' (pointing at Emily) 'got stranded cos this bitch zapped you with that thing and buggered off.'

'What!' Emily couldn't believe her ears. 'You can't honestly think I've had anything to do with *her*!'

'I don't believe in wild coincidences. No way could two lasses looking so similar just 'appen to bump into each other like you reckon. You obviously 'ad some sort of scam going on and fell out. I bet the two of you 'ave duped loads of poor lads like mine for money.'

Panic raced through Emily's body, realising Violet's

promise to let her go was a lie.

Violet told Emily: 'Before I knew about that bitch I was gonna drive *you* to a quiet road and run over you. You'd be just another 'it and run case.'

Emily's face went from red to white.

'You can't take such risks with Natalia from here.'

'You both need punishing. If we ain't come 'ome early Ricky would've been toast.'

'But I didn't –'

'This slut'll get run over now.' Violet nodded at Natalia. 'I'll mow you down in your ex-partner's Beamer, put her inside it, and arrange an accident.'

Emily's breathing speeded up.

'Don't shit yourself! I won't kill *you*. You might even get away with knocking down your fellow scammer. That said, you'll be stranded in an even more remote area than where I found you today – at night. Plus you'll feel shit after crashing. Nought will prove me or ma daughter ever saw either of you. Once Jane gets in we'll take you out separately.'

Natalia giggled.

'You won't be laughing when I've beaten the shit out of you. We'll see if you're smiling when I take that Beamer for a spin in your direction while you're moon-bathing in the middle of the road.'

'Your son might not be retarded but you are and – yes! Come at me now! See who does best! You are heavier than me but I am quicker. You are big and fat, I am young and fit. I will make you feel this. When you are stunned I will go. Emily, let us end this with her.'

Emily shook her head, though contemplated if it was worth taking the risk. Natalia was all about self-preservation. She wouldn't hurt anybody unless they got in her way. Supposing they did beat Violet by joining forces. Natalia would still want to disappear with Emily's suitcases and steal her car. She'd hardly run off without a fight. Emily may get stunned again. If so she'd wake up beside

Violet. Plus Jane would probably be there. No, siding with Natalia was not an option.

Emily glanced at the wall clock, feeling a rush of hope. Her boyfriend was due to visit between quarter past and half past five. The time was now five twenty. He'd never been late before.

Trying to keep herself focused, Emily asked Natalia why she hadn't gone sooner.

'At first I did need directions. Once I knew, I went to a shop to sell your necklace. I came here after this.'

'What's in my suitcases?'

'Your best clothes and jewellery.'

'Why have you waited around?'

'I felt hungry. After eating your food, I rang my cousin. The phone was busy. I did decide to rest for five minute on your bed but fell asleep for a long time. I spoke to my cousin on the phone twenty minute ago and was going to him when you came in.'

'So your cousin *does* live down this street.'

'No, but he live in Hull. I did not know his address, but have his phone number. When you turn back today I felt in danger, so wanted to learn where you live, phone my cousin from here, and steal some things. I saw from you skirt suit and necklace you have good, expensive taste in clothes and jewellery. Anyway, my cousin will drive me to York. If I am not at his house in five minute he will come here. It will take him no longer than ten minute. His girlfriend will come too.' Natalia looked at Violet. 'You should forget this. When they come here there will be three of us.'

'Jane'll be the first person through that door. Anyway, I think you've just spun a bullshit story to get me to leave.'

'I just want to go to York. I know an ugly man there who I do not like. I want to marry him. He is rich. If you let me walk out now without the fuss I will send you some money to say sorry for everything.'

'I'm surprised I can bloody breathe in 'ere with all this

verbal diarrhoea floating about.'

Natalia addressed Emily: 'She is too stupid to believe the truth. Help me rush this fat pig and I will let you keep your suitcases.'

'She's too stupid to *believe* the truth, but you're incapable of *speaking* the truth.'

They all began talking at once, only to fall silent upon hearing the front door open. No one had knocked beforehand.

Violet sneered. Natalia nodded. Emily gulped.

'Jane wouldn't 'ave bothered knocking.'

'I tell my cousin to walk in if the door is not locked.'

'I always leave it unlocked ten minutes before my boyfriend comes.'

They all raised their weapons as the living room door handle turned.

# WHERE'S WALTER

Robert entered the library and approached the helpdesk.

'Can I help?' said Walter the librarian.

'Do you have a copy of *Let's Go a-Fishing*, by A. Rehlwich?'

'I'll check the computer for you.'

'Thanks. No one's heard of –'

'Ah! You're in luck. There's a copy on the top floor. The lift –'

'Sorry to be a pest; lifts don't agree with me. I don't fancy going up all those flights of stairs either. Would you be so good as to send someone to fetch it?'

'I'll go myself, sir.' Walter walked out from behind the desk. 'Back in five minutes.'

Robert stood smiling as the librarian disappeared into the lift.

Fifteen minutes later he was still waiting.

Another librarian – Sarah – appeared behind the helpdesk. Did Robert need any assistance?

'I've just spent quarter of an hour waiting for one of your colleagues, who assured me he'd be back in five minutes, to fetch a book from the top floor.'

Sarah emerged from behind the helpdesk. She

promised not to be long as she headed for the lift. She returned from the top floor several minutes later with a ruffled brow.

'I've searched all over the top floor. Walter's nowhere to be seen. I did find this book lying open on a table though.' She showed it to Robert. 'Is this what you asked for?'

'Yes!' Robert took the book. 'That's it!'

Sarah strolled back behind the helpdesk.

'It's rather odd that your colleague – Walter, did you say his name was?'

'Yes.'

'It's rather odd that Walter's just vanished like that.'

'He's the fifth librarian to disappear over the last seven years.'

'Really? You don't think …'

'I don't know what to think, sir. Still, Walter may turn up yet.'

'Maybe there's a Bermuda Triangle-type of thing on the top floor?'

'Whatever it is, it hasn't affected any female staff. Only male workers have vanished – and I mean *vanished*. No one's ever seen or heard of them again.'

'Dear me! Let's hope Walter's okay.'


Robert walked home, mulling over the occurrences in the library. Walter's disappearance even took his mind off his much sought after book until he got settled in his living room. He flicked through the pages, stopping every so often to read snippets or study a picture.

In the centre of the book he discovered a two-page spread of an enchanting scene of a river flowing through a woodland area. Along the bank sat five fishermen casting their rods into the beautiful water.

'Wonderful scenery. Hang on … it *can't* be!' Robert checked the latest publishing date of the book. '1992!

That's twenty years ago!'

He turned back to the picture. One of the fishermen looked *exactly* like Walter.

'He's even wearing the same clothes! This is making me dizzy.'


Four hours later Robert's wife returned home. She entered the living room, noticing an open book on the coffee table.

'That's a lovely picture,' she said, admiring the photo of a river and six fishermen.

# ANT VALUES

We ants are misunderstood. Just because we're nasty, vicious little critters doesn't mean we don't deserve our place in the world. Just think of all the rubbish that we clear away. No one else can be bothered to do that. You won't see the beloved butterfly carrying objects away that are several times heavier than their own bodyweight. For us ants that's an easy task.

Next time you feel like cursing an ant, stop and think about wasps. Now they really are an abomination. We only attack humans if we feel threatened. Wasps will sting you just to satisfy their own sadistic pleasure. Wasps are nothing more than black and yellow flying turds. Whenever their kind buzzes into our territory we rip the evil buggers apart.

We ants could rid humankind of many irritations. You should be glad to share the world with us.

Don't abuse us – praise us.

# THE BEAUTY OF RAILINGS

Not being in any need for money after winning a large sum on the Spanish lottery last time I visited Prague, I answered an advert in the *Turbulent Times* newspaper that read:

*£10 an hour to whoever looks after my cat while I sod off to Southampton for ten days.*

Perhaps I should mention that I live in Scarborough, but to be honest, I'd rather not mention it.

I turned up at this house that was painted purple, apart from the door, which I ended up knocking on. Most likely no one will care what colour the door was, therefore I'll make a point of stating it was turquoise, except for the top panel, which was made from a rare substance called plywood. A pleasant picture was painted upon the plywood; a painting of a pink poodle wearing Porky Pig pants. Funny that, as I once owned a porky pig who wore pants portraying pictures of pink poodles peeing placidly in a park.

No one answered my knock. This would've offended me if I was a forty-one-year-old Serbian woman from

Hungary with a passion for radioactive white mice that don't like cheese unless it's been roasted for eight minutes under an unplugged grill. Luckily this wasn't an issue, yet something in the back of my old boat at the bottom of the River Nile told me never to knock on this door again for as long as stars shine and dinosaurs roam the earth.

My B-plan was to ring the doorbell, which I did, and it was covered in beeswax. Could've done without that. This reminded me of how much I hate tangerines. I don't really hate tangerines at all but tangerines make me think of tangerine candyfloss and tangerine candyfloss reminds me of my ex-girlfriend after seeing her naked for the second time.

A dwarf answered the door. I used to know a dwarf. His name was Sarah-Jane. This fellah's name was Apricot. He wore fingerless gloves on his feet and odd socks on his hands. I couldn't understand why the hell he didn't have a beard. Was he a vegan?

Apricot said, 'Round the back's me cat, pal. You're not allergic, are you, pal?'

'Yes,' I said (for Apricot was addressing me whenever he said 'pal'), 'I'm allergic to zebras and popcorn, but the latter only bothers me when covered in seagull dust.'

Apricot locked the front door and led me round the back way. I could tell you why he didn't make life easier by taking me through the house, but can't be bothered to remark on this subject any more than yellow sweaters can complement Russian lasagne. I may make mention of the massive mauve manikin of a mighty military man and the cream-coloured cactus-shaped Victorian water fountain, built in Georgian times, which we passed on our way round the side of the house, though such matters require serious thought before, well, you know.

''Ere's me fat cat, pal,' said the beardless dwarf as we entered the kitchen.

I got quite a surprise. The cat lay on his back guzzling from a bottle of Cointreau that he held in his four paws.

Although it may seem obvious that he should have four paws, think on this: what if he'd been involved in a shipping accident? Ah yes! The thing that surprised me was that the cat was black and white – I didn't think such a cool combination of colours could occur. What next, one may wonder? A grey elephant?

Apricot snatched the Cointreau from the uniquely-marked cat and, in a tone of voice not heard in England since the Napoleonic War of the Roses, said, 'You fat twat! I told you to keep off after last time. 'Ee once drank a full bottle, pal, leaving me nought but water to put on me cornflakes for breck'ast. I'm sodding off now, pal. Cat's called Rover.'

Apricot sodded off, leaving me with Rover, who staggered to one end of the kitchen. To be fair, he wasn't likely to stagger to two ends of the kitchen at the same time. Just like in the famous Aesop Fairy Tale, written by the Brothers Grim, the cat shat on the mat. The smell was a mixture of cat crap and Cointreau, as anyone with an articulated grasp of physics will know. Rover fainted, reminding me of the time I injected wine into my bloodstream. I don't know why this memory was brought forth though, so don't ask me to explain.

Apricot's house was unusual. Those of you with a sense of curiosity will probably be wondering what was unusual about it. Well this is where readers' imagination kicks in. Statements like this take me back to the year before I was born when everything was an adventure and nothing was what nothing is. This type of thing should not be confused with the more common occurrence of goat watching.

My first eight days at Apricot's house zoomed past like a mere 192 hours. The tenth hour of the ninth day found me stood outside facing the field backing on to the garden. In theory I should've mentioned that Apricot's house was situated in the back of beyond, but I've had nose-ache until this exact moment.

A fish pond resided near the field. Rover didn't like this pond as it contained no fish. I disliked it as it was devoid of water, meaning I had to wash my hands at the kitchen or bathroom sink before meals and after extractions. On the plus side, just behind the pond, backing onto the field, stood some railings. Black railings made of metal, four feet high, spreading eight feet wide. Why was this on the plus side, I hear no one ask? I'll tell you: I'm passionate about railings. Every day I sat on the back doorstep with Rover, sharing a bottle of Cointreau, admiring these beautiful railings.

At about eleven minutes past noon on my last day of catsitting, a raven-coloured raven landed near the railings. Now before any smart-arse says, 'Oi! Numb nuts! What other colour would a raven be, eh?' let me say this: three green-coloured ravens flapped by me three times in the last three months. On one occasion a red raven crossed my path with silver, though the red raven was a rapist, recently released for righting several really revolting wrongs. Regarding the red raven being a rapist, I rightly reckon it would be really wrong to relate to her after what she did to that heartbroken hedgehog from Haworth.

Anyway, this raven-coloured raven started raving near the railings. I looked at Rover for his response. He burped, adjusted his collar and tie, took a drink of Cointreau, and burped again. I asked the raven-coloured raven why he was raving near the railings.

'What's it to you, you funnel-nosed tosser!' said the raven-coloured raven, raving on.

You could have bowled me over with a sixpence: a rude raven.

Apricot showed up bang on time, albeit he was three minutes late. I warned him not to walk on the bats for we all know what would happen if he did, don't we? If not, look online for the most infamous event that happened in the twenty-first century, two days after June the 1st of July 1898.

The second thing I said to Apricot was, 'Can't remember.' Reason being, he asked if I knew the German word for 'trypophobia'. Although I was taught French when I wasn't at school this was one German word that'd flown from my memory bank like a penguin flying from its nest for the first time.

After not thanking me for burying a mango in his garden, Apricot asked whether I'd had any problems. I said my only problems had taken place before he'd met me, which didn't interest him, much to my amazement.

Once Apricot had paid me I told him about the raven-coloured raven I'd seen raving near the railings.

'I've seen that twat afore, pal. It called me a bald-faced tosser. No need for it, pal.'

I exchanged raised eyebrows with Apricot, shook hands with Rover, took another photo of those beautiful railings, told that raven-coloured raven to sod off when he appeared like a stork delivering a baby and started raving in front of the railings again, just as I was about to drop a penny in the pond for good luck, and ...

Sorry, had to pause there. My previous sentence was so sodding long, I couldn't recall where I was heading with it. Still can't, for that matter ...

Okay, better admit defeat and give up on that last scene. Think it had something to do with leaving Rover's kitchen. Anyway, here we are, back on the train. By 'we' I mean me and my new grey cat. Sorry if that sounded like I was including you in my 'we'. My new grey cat is called Shep. We met at the train station. He reminded me of someone I didn't meet two years earlier in a pub that ran out of draft cocoa. If you believe that's hard to believe, believe me, I found it unbelievable at the time. Luckily I wasn't hungry otherwise it would've been a serious issue for the lost sheep of Alcatraz.

Now I'm here with Shep, happy in Hayley Hollers Hotel in Halifax. Not sure why we stopped here to be honest, though as it's nearly midnight and we're about twenty-one miles from wherever we're going next, there's no real harm in us finding a bed for the night – a bed for Shep, that is. Obviously I'll stretch out on the floor.

As we fancied a couple of drinks before settling down to rest, we had a couple of drinks before settling down to rest. Whilst sat at the bar, consuming copious quantities of Cointreau, keeping a keen eye on the capacious-bosomed serving wench, a raven-coloured raven roamed in and started raving on about some railings he'd been raving near. I invited him to join us, so he joined us. We relished raving on about the beauty of railings until Shep became really ravenous.

# SPLATTERED

I am Marek. I am come from a country called Slovakia, which is far from England. I am tonight going to some pubs with my new English girlfriend. Her name it is Eve. She have brown hair that hang almost to her sexy bum. She have the greatest glass-hour body in the entire UK and most of Europe. Eve have the beautifulist face ever I have seen. Her forehead is the best part of her, I think. She have glasses to help her see and lips tasting better than raspberry jam. She always wear the short skirts and the tall heels. Her personality is okay.


It's Eve here, as you no doubt can tell, as I'm neither stupid nor ugly. I suspect Marek's been hanging out here, talking to you, probably confusing the hell out of you. Well pay him no heed. He's like a dog on heat, though I suspect you gathered that. Take no offence and I apologise if he praised me for my beauty or compared me to raspberry jam. I realise you know this already. I – oh! I've just gone redder than a baboon's bottom! I thought I was talking to Kay. Sorry to bother you. I have to get ready now. Bye!

Marek tended to leave things to the last minute. Eight o'clock came and went when he realised he'd ran out of deodorant. Luckily vanilla-scented air freshener made a fine substitute. Eve, meanwhile, waited at the pub, wearing a sexy dress and a frown upon her face. Better late than never, she thought, when her muscular Marek swaggered into the pub. Although maybe it was better never than late. When the Slovakian stud passed through the glass doors, a car full of criminals on the run from the law thundered in behind him and …

Kay said, 'If only Marek hadn't stopped to pick up those three 2 pence pieces from the floor, which that student had been tossing, then he would've been sat with you, and not crushed by that Volvo. What a cruel world we live in, Eve! By the way, I do like your dress. Is it new?'

'Thanks. Yes, it is new. It wasn't cheap, either. I'll miss Marek. Fancy going to Aldi?' 'Ooh! That reminds me: this morning I saw Rowan Atkinson sketching a fetching sketch of the fetching Sophia Bush, fetching a bucket of water from a well – Who do I ring?'

# ARRABELLA WELLFITT

Arrabella sat on a blue chair, wearing a blue dress, in a blue mood, wondering what colour the sea would be if it wasn't blue. The living room she occupied was decorated in blue too, apart from the ceiling, though turquoise is really just a poor man's blue, if you think about it. Even if you don't think about it, like Arrabella wasn't, the theory still exists. Her mother always warned her that if she didn't learn how to decorate, she wouldn't be able to decorate. Sounds simple enough advice, but was it?

The telephone rang. Arrabella decided to answer it, considering the phone was conveniently situated on the desk beside her. She was a writer, you see, hence the blue mood: writer's block.

It was the wrong number. If Arrabella ever used bad language, she would have used bad language now, but she didn't ever use bad language, therefore she didn't use it now. Another thing she couldn't say was Hexakosioihexekontahexaphobia. Thankfully she didn't need to say this, as she had no fear of the number 666, though she believed the world would be a better place without those three digits strung together in sequence.

Rather than using foul language, she told the man – for there was no doubting the deep voice on the other end of the phone belonged to a member of the rougher sex – not to worry. She didn't mind having her day intruded upon by a complete stranger wanting to know if Baz was home.

The deep voice responded, stating that he was not a *complete* stranger.

In a haughty tone Arrabella said, 'What do you mean, you're not a "complete" stranger? How could you be otherwise?'

'Although we've never spoken before, I recognise your haughty tone.'

'Excuse me?'

'I said –'

'Yes, yes, yes! I'm not deaf! How can you recognise my – and I'm not haughty, by the way – how can –'

'Are you Arrabella Wellfitt?'

'Why, yes! Who is this?'

'Leo Ardhass. We walked past each other one sunny day. You were on your mobile. That's how I recognise your voice. You said to the person on the other end, "Just about enough".'

'When was this? I don't re –'

'Seven weeks, six days ago. You were wearing a blue dress, like what you're wearing today. Don't worry, I can't see you now – though I wish I could – I saw you in Fleecer's this morning.'

Fleecer's was a shop in the nearby village of Scrattem.

'Well I've heard "just about enough" of this creepy conversation! Don't ever ring me again, you – you *stalker*!'

Arrabella slammed the phone down.

She suspected that Leo Ardhass didn't call her home number by accident. As a child, she had learned origami, thus giving her enhanced intuition when untoward matters are hovering in the wind. And outside it was blowing a gale.

How long had this deep-voiced weirdo been watching her? Being a desirable young girl of twenty-eight, living alone in a detached house, a mile from the nearest village, semi-famous for having an article about cabbages published in *Know Veg, Grow Veg* magazine last year, she decided that a phone call to her boyfriend was in order.

Something seemed different when she heard Gregory Conner – her other half – talk to her via mobile phone. He spoke in a pre-break-up tone of voice before declaring he was jealous of her semi-fame; sick of her having more time for writing than for him; tired of awestruck people treating her like royalty whenever they went to Scrattem, yet they never acknowledged him, the man holding her hand. On top of all this, he'd met a girl with little intelligence, who – although nowhere near as gorgeous as the gorgeous Arrabella, renowned for being gorgeous – did whatever he wanted to do, whenever he wanted to do it, including cutting the fingernails of his right hand – a task Arrabella always avoided – which he cannot achieve without spilling tears.

Arrabella hung up on him. Not because he'd dumped her, but due to his, 'It'll be all right, don't fuss about it' response when she related her earlier phone call with Leo.

Suddenly she remembered she'd forgotten to eat a pear. Arrabella maintained her exquisite figure by undertaking regular exercise and eating small amounts of food every two or three hours.

As she glided into the kitchen like she owned the place, the smell of brown rice brought back memories of her morning trip to Fleecer's. Not many customers were around with it being before 9 *ante meridiem* on a Tuesday.

Arrabella sat upon the kitchen worktop, taking care not to ladder her tights on any uncooked grains of rice she'd dropped earlier, but hadn't made time to clear away. This may sound overcautious to some people, yet Arrabella would be quick to tell all doubters to never underestimate the power of uncooked grains of rice.

She bit into the ripe pear, commencing a tour of her memory bank. No male faces came to mind from her shopping trip, but then why would they? She was there to buy rice and various other stuff, not hunt for a man. Besides, at that time she had a boyfriend.

A man she thought she knew didn't want her, while another she didn't know did. She felt no regret for splitting up with Gregory. They'd only been an item for three months. Besides, self-obsessed men had never appealed to her, even if they did have a big dictionary she could borrow. He'd seemed okay when they first met, but over time he became more and more like a whining six-year-old girl, wanting constant attention and a pony for Christmas.

Arrabella slid off the worktop without ripping her tights to shreds on renegade grains of rice, deposited the pear-core into the little food-waste caddy, washed her hands, and said aloud, 'If someone said make a wish, I would wish for Leo to give my ex-boyfriend two black eyes in the presence of a handsome policeman, who'd arrest Leo or at least caution him. If he bothered me after that the police would know he was dodgy and would take me seriously if I reported him for stalking. Now I really must stop talking to myself.'

Arrabella returned to her desk, upon which resided her laptop, currently displaying a blank page.

She was also a freelance proofreader. A client was due to email her a document today, containing their new book about the history of codpieces and why they are no longer fashionable. Arrabella went online. Whilst waiting for the page to load, she picked off a loose hair from the hem of her dress, contemplating that the last time she'd worn this garment was when Leo saw her talking on the phone.

She remembered now: she wore her blue dress at a vegetable show held in the historic East Yorkshire town of Beverley. The only time she'd walked any distance was from her car, parked in the town centre, to the building hosting the event, which took less than five minutes. Did that mean Leo followed her everywhere?

Arrabella checked her emails. The expected message hadn't arrived, however, a second email from another potential client had. This one was from a woman called Rita Wheatear, from Scrattem, requiring a 50,000-word manuscript about unicorns proofreading. Unlike most of Arrabella's clients, Rita wanted her work checking in hardcopy format, not on-screen. She'd already printed it off. Could she bring the manuscript to Arrabella or would Arrabella rather come to Scrattem?

They decided to meet in the village café at 2 *post meridiem*, giving Arrabella time to brush her flowing locks of nut-brown hair and apply a touch of red to her divine lips; lips that so many wished to kiss after seeing the gorgeous writer's photo accompanying her cabbage article. She switched the radio on whilst undertaking these essential tasks.

The first thing that came on the radio was a news report about purple carrots, reminding Arrabella of rabbits, which in turn made her think of a specific hare, while she brushed her hair. She emitted a mirthless laugh, surprised that brushing her hair didn't immediately remind her of the hare in her nightmare. This hare of hers was no ordinary hare.

The last few nights she'd had a recurring dream about being lost in the middle of nowhere, traipsing along a county back road, with nothing but yellow fields at either side, stretching for miles and miles, until she finally catches a lift from a tractor driver, who lets her sit on the back of his trailer. The tractor moves along at a speed slower that an asthmatic snail with a bullfrog on its back.

Suddenly, in the dream, a large hare appears on the road, several feet from the back of the trailer. The hare's emerald eyes are mesmerising. For a while it follows the slow-moving vehicle, never taking its eyes off Arrabella, who is always attired in her blue dress. At length the hare changes into a cat and leaps up onto the trailer. The grinning feline nuzzles Arrabella's pert nose.

All of a sudden she's lying on a grass bank. The tractor and trailer have vanished, along with her clothes, though she isn't left stark-naked: she's attired in a bikini made from cabbage leaves. The cat is stretched out beside her. As soon as it starts talking about fly-fishing, Arrabella always wakes up in a cold sweat.

Back in reality, Arrabella slotted on a pair of three-inch heels, grabbed her handbag, and headed for the front door. Needless to say, her expression altered for the worst after stepping outside to discover a man wearing a hare's head, crouching – like a hare – in front of the garage. The hare's head was part of a man-sized costume. No doubt existed in Arrabella's mind that it was a hare, for the ears were too long to be those of a little bunny rabbit.

'Don't worry,' said the hare-man, straightening up, 'I just want your autograph.'

They stood about ten feet apart. Arrabella didn't know whether to scream, run, faint, charge, pray, or whistle 'Dixie'. Her trance was broken when the hare-man produced an A4-sized photo from a satchel hanging from his shoulder.

Arrabella pointed at him with her finger, as that's the part of her anatomy she prefers pointing with, although she has been known to point with her foot, if her arms are folded, while watching TV with someone.

'You're Leo What's-his-name!'

Arrabella stopped pointing at this point, for she could see no point in pointing any longer, now that she'd made her point.

'No, I'm Leo Ardhass. After our phone call, I thought it'd be okay to visit.'

'Why are you wearing the head from a hare costume?'

'In case you thought I was a serial murderer, currently on the run from the Labour Party for using a gold bracelet to kill seventeen gorgeous blondes, thus making you phone the KGB, who'd wrongly arrest me for urinating in a public place. Sign this photo and I'll go.'

Leo stepped closer. Arrabella outstretched one arm, raising her hand in a stop sign. She would only ever perform this type of action with her hand. Even if she was sat watching TV with someone, arms folded, she'd never use her foot as a stop sign.

'Don't come near me! Put it down over there then step back to where you are now.'

Arrabella pointed to the far side of the wide driveway, indicating where to leave the picture.

Leo complied, dropping a pebble from the drive on top to prevent the photo blowing away in the gale-type weather, though to be fair, the winds were easing now. He returned to his spot in front of the garage straight after this event.

Arrabella slinked towards the photo like a paranoid lioness, never taking her eyes off Leo, until she returned to her original position. She inspected the image.

'Where did you get this?'

The shot was not of the accompanying picture featured with her article on cabbages, as she'd suspected, but one taken two months ago. The image showed her attired in the dress she presently wore, holding a parsnip.

'No photos were taken of me at the vegetable show! No one's heard of me in the historic East Yorkshire town of Beverley. You followed me! *You* took this picture! Don't come any closer!'

'Yes, I took it! Ever since you stirred my soul with that beautiful article about cabbages, and your gorgeous picture melted my heart into a thousand streams, I've been like a man possessed! How I've longed to kiss those divine lips of yours! Secretly, I collected any information in the local paper about you, following you wherever I could, and was unable to resist taking photos of you at that vegetable show. Gorgeous Arrabella! Will you marry me?'

Leo's wiry frame shook all over as he dropped on one knee. Arrabella also shook, but for different reasons. How should she edge her way out of this situation without inciting trouble?

Plan A: 'This has taken me by surprise. I'll consider it while I go see a client in –'

'Rita Wheatear!' Leo shot to his feet. 'She only exists inside my head, like Baz. I got your email from your website. Don't worry, I can still get you some work. I've written ninety-three love poems about you.'

Plan B: 'That'll keep me busy. Wait here while I fetch a pen to sign this parsnip – erm, photo.'

As she stepped back, he rushed forwards, taking something from the satchel. Arrabella was poised to scream – not that anyone would hear; it just seemed appropriate – though refrained from doing so when a pen was thrust into her raised hand.

Plan C: if this nut was thinking of kidnapping her, raping her, killing her, or marrying her, he might lose confidence if deprived of his hare-head. In a flash, Arrabella seized the huge ears and whipped off the disguise. Now she couldn't help screaming: underneath Leo wore a plastic facemask of a grinning cat.

Arrabella raced inside, locking the door behind her, relieved that he didn't try grabbing her. What would happen next? Would he start talking through the letterbox about fly-fishing, promising only to stop if she danced in front of him attired in a cabbage bikini? Arrabella froze as the letterbox snapped. His voice filled her ears, creating excess wax, informing her he'd just posted the photo.

'You can keep my pen, but please sign the picture. I'll wait outside till you've done it. By the way, about my proposal; I know it's a bit sudden, but I'm happy to have a long engagement. I don't mind living together for a few years if that'd help you say yes. I look forward to us taking our little Jamie and Amy to the park when they're old enough to toddle.'

Arrabella phoned the police.

\*

Half an hour later, when the cat-hare – or hare-cat, depending on your preference – had been arrested, a policeman informed Arrabella that Leo Ardhass had spent most of his life in mental institutions. He'd been released last year when all but one ailment had been cured. The doctors felt confident that his remaining problem would never be an issue. He'd been obsessed with the idea of marrying a beautiful writer – preferably with flowing nut-brown hair – possessing an adept knowledge of cabbages. Even Arrabella admitted that the chances of him discovering such a person were one in ten million. Typical that she should be that one.

Arrabella returned to her desk the following day. Laptop on, writer's block gone. Somehow yesterday's events had inspired her creativity.

# RASPBERRIES

My name's Vicky, short for Victoria. I'm a twenty-year-old female girl or woman with long auburn hair. Some people say it's ginger, but it's not. Ginger is a light reddish-yellow colour. Auburn is a reddish-brown colour. My hair doesn't have any yellow in it at all.

I work afternoons cleaning at an old peoples' home. I like all wildlife except for rats and wasps, because rats can make you ill by giving you the plague and wasps sting people for no reason. Sometimes I get things mixed up, but don't know why. Once when I was ten I called a dandelion a daisy. Getting mixed up often causes me to forget things, especially in the morning when I don't always remember what day it is. This forgetfulness has been a problem all my life, like on my eighth birthday, when I couldn't remember how to spell yeeste.

I have the same thing for breakfast every morning: a glass of Ribena, two pieces of toast spread with jam, and seven raspberries. By always having this meal it reminds me what to buy from the shops. How awful would it be to come down for breakfast and only have meatballs, potatoes, asparagus, and green beans to eat? That's my usual meal for when I get home from work at about twenty-one minutes past five.

The day before last Tuesday I wondered what would happen at breakfast if there were fewer than seven raspberries in my fridge. This would probably leave me feeling hungry until lunch time unless I rushed to the shops like a great hound chasing a heron and bought more raspberries. After spending half an hour and ten minutes imagining what might happen I searched through my phone book for local fortune tellers. The one who seemed to be the best was called Gallantevo.

I searched through my phone book for local fortune – oh! – I've already said that! I forget things sometimes, but don't know why. Once when I was seventeen I bought some carrots because I'd forgotten I don't like them. Anyway, I went to see Gallantevo the fortune teller. He was a male boy or man aged about forty-one.

Gallantevo said, 'If you run out of raspberries on Wednesday –'

'No – sorry – I want to know what would happen if I ran out of them *tomorrow*.'

'Tomorrow *is* Wednesday.'

With me getting my days mixed up sometimes I was sure tomorrow was Tuesday. After four minutes of talking about what day it was, Gallantevo made me realise he was right, as yesterday I'd watched a programme about wildebeest migraine. I really like wildlife apart from rats and wasps and love watching TV programmes about animals.

Where was I? Oh yes! Gallantevo said if there were no raspberries left on Wednesday, and if I *didn't* race to the shop like a rabbit with a sprocket on his or her back, I'd get tennis elbow. This confused me. I've never played tennis. At school we played netball, though I wasn't any good at it. When the best girls picked sides they always left me till last. They said I was too small and useless. After telling Gallantevo this he said anyone who's played netball could still get a bad elbow when they're older. Maybe he really meant I'd get netball elbow.

Gallantevo said, 'If you run out of raspberries and you *do* go to the shop, you'll meet a tall, dark, handsome stranger.'

'But I don't know any strangers.'

'£50.'

'What is? The stranger?'

Gallantevo confused me. He wanted me to pay him £50, which seemed quite cheap.

Not having any real friends, I decided to run out of raspberries and go to the shop. I bought a carton (of raspberries, not milk) and waited outside the store for six hours and fourteen minutes. No one even said hello to me. I went away feeling disappointed, but glad it didn't rain.

When I got back to my street, lots of police officers and firemen were there. This surprised me, especially when most of them were stood outside my house. A tall male policeman told me to keep clear because a fire had just been put out. I started crying, saying it was my home that had been burnt.

The policeman was very kind. He took me to my grandparents' house. I gave him three raspberries for helping me. Later, a female policewoman told me an escaped prisoner had stolen a car and – after being chased by the police – crashed it into my home about nine minutes after I went out. The car, already on fire, exploded when it hit my door. My living room was all burnt. I felt lucky, remembering that this day was the first morning in about two years and eleven months that I went out during that time.

I stayed with my grandparents for thirteen days. After this I was re-housed. My new home was okay, apart from having damp patches in both bedrooms and torn, dirty, awful-looking lino on the kitchen floor. Luckily there weren't any rats crawling under the floorboards or wasps buzzing around in the windows.

I wanted to have a housewarming party but apart

from my grandparents there wasn't anyone else I knew well enough to ask. When I was six I went to Wendy Wuffle's seventh birthday party at her house. What's funny is that whilst there I ate my first raspberry and didn't like it. I ate my second one by accident at Samantha Spriteworthy's ninth birthday party, really loved the taste, and have done ever since. My dream job would be running my own raspberry farm. This would be difficult to do though, as I've never been to college and don't know how to grow plants.

Although there's more to say about my life, I must go. The reason why is that I've just switched on the telly to watch a programme about insects. I'd forgotten it was on until now and an awful flock of wasps are buzzing round a lonely girl or woman trying to eat from her carton of raspberries.

# CASH 'N' CARROTS

A flash of auburn hair shot past Emma's window. What did I do to deserve a neighbour like Vicky? she thought, stepping outside, locking the door behind her.

Vicky rose from her crouching position near the bins. Her smile disappeared when Emma warned her not to run into her garden whenever she felt like it. Vicky – aged twenty – was only three years younger than Emma, yet she was reprimanded like a child being told off by its mother.

'Sorry. I was calling to – oh look!' She pointed at the bins. 'There he is again!' Emma stepped back in case 'he' was a spider. 'It's a butterfly! Isn't he lovely?'

Vicky's eyes were like saucers. She had an almost permanent 'stare'.

'He's flying away now. Bye, bye, butterfly!'

Emma fixed her dark tresses into a ponytail as she walked a tightrope line down the path. She opened the gate, indicating for Vicky to step out first. They faced each other in their narrow lane, which divided four houses on either side.

Vicky asked Emma if she wanted any peaches.

'Peaches?'

'They're a type of fruit.'

'I know what they are, for goodness' sake!'

'Well, my grandma gave me some. I don't like them, but thought with you being really fit and healthy you might want them.'

'Peaches are the only fruit I don't like, to be honest.'

'Never mind. Just thought I'd ask.'

Emma noted Vicky's bowed head and disappointed tone of voice.

'It was kind of you to offer, though.'

Vicky looked up, smiling.

'Anyway, must go.' Emma began walking away, but stopped to ask: 'Why did you accept the peaches if you didn't want them?'

'My grandparents don't like peaches but didn't want to waste them.'

'And they thought you liked them?'

'No, they know I don't.'

'Hmph! So why did your grandmother buy the peaches in the first place?'

'Because they were cheap.'

'Goodbye, Vicky!'

Emma's high heels clacked against the concrete and her ponytail swished from side to side as she hastened down the lane.

The women lived down Appleby Avenue in Hull, with Emma at Number 1, Vicky at Number 5. Their lane emerged onto a bigger road called Cobble Street where Emma parked her red BMW. She didn't notice the Land Rover at the opposite side of the road until the driver stepped out of the vehicle, calling her name. She turned to see Thomas, an estate agent from Badby's who let out most of the properties down Appleby Avenue, including Emma's and Vicky's.

Thomas wandered over, hands in pockets, eyes smiling at the shortness of Emma's skirt and the capacious bosom straining against her suit jacket.

'Can't talk now, Thomas.'

'No worries. Just came for Vicky's rent. Do you know if she's in?'

'She is at the moment. I think she starts work at noon.'

'Does she still clean in that old codgers' 'ome?'

'Think so.' Emma adjusted her glasses before opening the car door. 'Got to go.'

She sat in the driving seat when Thomas enquired if she fancied having a drink with him that evening.

'Maybe. Don't know right now.'

'Think about it. I'll call you later.'

Neither Emma nor Thomas noticed the large bearded figure, wearing overalls and a cap, watching them from the end of Cobble Street.

Emma thought about Thomas's request during her drive through Hull to the factory. She'd known him for about a year. He was good-looking yet there was something smug about him. Emma hadn't been on a date for months. This was not because nobody was interested in her, for she had legions of admirers, but her increased workload since her boss's departure left her too tired for socialising. Emma's only romantic interest was in one of her neighbours: a twenty-something Slovakian who'd recently moved into the house opposite her. They'd bumped into each other several times when Emma was returning from work or from the shops. They hadn't stopped to introduce each other properly but always exchanged greetings in passing.

The more Emma considered Thomas's offer the less she liked the idea. The estate agent's dodgy smugness stuck in her mind more than his handsome appearance.

On top of Emma being distracted by Vicky and Thomas this morning, she was also delayed by slow-moving traffic, resulting in her arriving at work ten minutes late. She hurried through the factory door, punching her card into the clocking-in machine. All fifteen beauty-product packers turned round as she rushed past quicker than usual.

Emma collided into her co-worker as she barged through the main office door.

'Sorry, Bella!'

'Just assault me, why don't you!'

'Don't be absurd! You know it was an accident.'

Bella scowled. She'd never forgiven Emma after Mr Twaddle made her responsible for most of the managerial duties since the two of them were left to run the business until the new manager takes over. When the former head of the firm retired, his replacement – Mr Splatterworth – fell off his son's skateboard, twisting his ankle, the day before he was due to start work.

'Well you're late today. The manager's phone's rung twice.'

'Damn! It's all that stupid Vicky's fault for delaying me in the first place!'

Emma sat down, grabbed the manager's phone, and checked the last caller's number. In Mr Splatterworth's absence she'd spent most of her time at his desk.

'Hmph! I don't recognise it.'

She dug out a file from one of the tall cabinets.

After checking the number Emma had written down, Bella said, 'It was Mr Splatterworth who rang.'

'What!'

'That's right. You would've known if you were here on time. He called my phone after trying the one in *your* office. He's coming in today. You'd better move all your stuff out of here before he arrives.'

'Of all the days to be late!'

'If he's anything like Mr Rankbotham he won't approve of you wearing pink.'

Their former boss expected his office staff to wear black or grey skirt suits, believing these colours looked more professional. One day Emma came in wearing red. Mr Rankbotham sent her home to change, threatening to dock her wages if she didn't abide by his rules, adding that he'd once sacked a lady for coming to work attired in pink.

He had recommended the new manager to Mr Twaddle for his replacement. Emma suspected Mr Splatterworth would be of the same mould as his predecessor, yet daren't risk going home to change after being late. Surely her attendance mattered more than her appearance? Plus she'd done a great job in the new boss's absence.

After clearing her personal items from the manager's office, Emma – seated at her own desk – felt unable to settle down to work. She kept glancing at the door every few seconds, expecting Mr Splatterworth to barge through, giving her a verbal warning.

Ten thirty was Emma's five-minute break time. She found it hard to enjoy her Stayslim cereal bar this morning.

A knock on the door startled her. Mr Splatterworth entered just as Emma deposited the cereal bar wrapper into the bin.

'Keeping the place tidy, I see. I'm Shane Splatterworth, the new manager.'

Emma walked over, arm outstretched.

'Pleased to meet you, Mr Splatterworth.'

'Call me Shane.' They shook hands. 'You must be Emma.'

'Yes, sir.'

'Less of the "sir". It's Shane.'

Emma had expected another Mr Rankbotham. A boss with an aura of gloom and doom who would've docked her pay if she ever called him by his first name. Instead here was a good-looking gent in his forties who knew how to smile. He had a relaxed attitude and wasn't even wearing a tie. On top of this he'd arrived at work two and a half hours late.

'Is there anything I can do for you, Mr Splat – Shane?'

'Hmmm, now there's a question! Ha, ha!'

'Do you want to check any specific files?'

'Good grief! Not at this early hour on a Monday! No, I'm just having a look round the place, finding out who's who, who does what. You will've heard that the day before I was supposed to start here I went arse over elbow when I fell off my son's skateboard. Anyway, what time did Mr Rankbotham start work?'

'Seven thirty.'

'Seven thirty! Sod that for a lark! What's the point in being a manager if you have to get up at the crack of dawn? Do you start at nine?'

'Yes.' Emma blushed. 'I must confess to being ten minutes late today because –'

'Well don't do it again or else I'll keep you in detention – ha, ha! Okay, I'll come in at about nine next week.'

'Will I still be needed to work an extra hour every night now your back, Mr – Shane?'

'Hell no! Forgot you'd been working till six every night. Five o'clock finishes from now on, though would you mind doing one last Saturday morning tomorrow?'

Mr Rankbotham would never have asked Emma if she 'minded' doing anything. With him it had always been 'Do this, do that.' Shane Splatterworth even thanked her for agreeing to come in tomorrow after she'd assented to his request.

Shane was halfway through the door when he stopped to say, 'By the way, I like your outfit. Good to see someone in bright colours for a change. I know you ladies like wearing something different every day, but just for once, dress the same tomorrow. I hate working Saturday mornings. My first one might be a little more bearable with a splash of pink brightening the place up.'

Emma was happy to oblige. Besides, she had two pink outfits. She'd wear the paler one tomorrow.

A rush of relief swept through her. She'd phone her sister Hayley later to ask if she fancied going out on

Saturday night.

Hayley had been with Emma when she'd first met Vicky. The sisters had returned to Appleby Avenue one day after a shopping trip. One of Emma's carrier bags split open near her house. Vicky – having stepped outside at the same time – came over to help gather up the scattered cans of vegetables. Since then Vicky kept *trying* to make friends.

What irritated Emma more than anything was when – on the odd occasion – Vicky called in to see her at work … like at eleven that morning.

Emma – sat working at her computer – glanced up when the door opened. Vicky entered with a carrier bag swinging from one hand.

'I hope you don't mind me –'

'Yes, I *do* mind.' Emma removed her glasses and rubbed her eyes. 'I've told you enough times not to bother me here.'

She replaced her specs and continued typing.

Vicky remained silent with unblinking eyes like green-centred moons. She resembled an obedient child waiting to be addressed.

'Will you please go? And don't come back ever again. I wish to goodness I'd never told you where I work. You must waste half an hour walking here.'

'It takes twenty-seven minutes from home, but if I walk from –'

'Vicky!' Emma raised her hands to the sides of her head. 'I don't care!' She began typing again without looking up as she spoke. 'Why don't you search for another part-time job instead of bothering me? The manger's back now. Goodness knows what he'll say if he catches you in here. It's obvious you're not a client. Just – damn! I'm making spelling mistakes now because of you!'

'Sorry.' Vicky's voice had become shaky, tears welled in her eyes. 'It's just that my grandma gave me –'

'I don't have time for this. Just leave and let me get on!'

'Sorry. I thought –'

'No, you never think. You act on impulse. If you dropped your mobile phone in a lions' den you'd march straight in to rescue it.'

'I don't have a mobile phone.'

'Close the door on your way out, please.'

Vicky left with teary eyes.

Five minutes later another knock came. As the door opened, Emma looked up from her PC, half-expecting to see Vicky again. Instead her co-worker approached her desk.

'What do you want, Bella? I'm busy.'

Bella placed Vicky's carrier bag on the desk.

'That strange little woman with the scary eyes left this with me. I shouldn't think Mr Splatterworth will be too keen on your friends visiting you at work.'

'She's not my friend, she's my neighbour.' Emma kept her eyes on the screen as she spoke. 'I've told that stupid girl before now to stop coming here. She drives me crazy with all her nonsense.'

'I don't think you'll have that worry for much longer.' Bella hovered in the doorway. 'Mr Splatterworth's giving her a warning by the looks of it. Don't be surprised if he has a go at you later for inviting her here.'

Emma looked up in time to catch Bella's cocky grin before she closed the office door. Moments later another knock came. Shane Splatterworth entered.

'I've – no need to stand, Emma – I've been talking to your friend Vicky –'

'Sorry about her. She's not –'

'Nothing to be sorry about. Vicky looked upset. I asked what was wrong. Said she was just being silly. We got talking. She told me about her job. Can you believe this? My Great Aunt Maud lives in the old folks' home where Vicky cleans! Anyway, you'll be pleased to know I've given her a job here. Vicky, that is – not Great Aunt Maud, ha, ha!'

Emma felt like she'd been encased in ice and frozen to her seat. She didn't hear Shane's next few words. At length she interrupted him.

'Excuse me, Mr Splatterworth, but –'

'Shane.'

'Shane – but what did you mean by giving Vicky a job here? She's not very bright.'

'You don't need to be a rocket scientist to clean toilets.'

'Ah. I thought you meant she'd be joining the production staff and be here all day.'

'You must have wax in your ear, my dear, ha, ha! I just told you that Vicky'll work half an hour from nine every morning. Bella said the usual cleaner can only come in between half one and two. Toilets should be cleaned twice a day … Vicky mentioned you two live down the same street.'

'That's the only reason we know each other.'

'Good. You'll be able to give her lift in. I don't mind if she stops to chat with you for five minutes after she's finished cleaning. I know you'll still get the job done.'

Emma somehow managed to resist the urge to scream. Now she was guaranteed to see Vicky at least five times a week, early in the morning.


Vicky left Twaddle Beauty Products with mixed emotions. She felt upset that yet another attempt to befriend Emma had backfired, but she'd perked up following her conversation with Shane. The extra cash she'd earn for cleaning the toilets would come in handy. Ever since moving to Appleby Avenue Vicky had found it hard to make ends meet. As she always fared badly in job interviews it was a stroke of luck bumping into Shane. Apart from her grandparents, not many people were friendly towards her like he'd been, thus making her look forward to the new job even more. Better still, she'd get more opportunities to build a friendship with Emma, now that they'd see each other five mornings a week. Her past attempts at making friends with people always went wrong, though she spent too much time alone to stop trying.

Over the last five years Vicky's only social time revolved around visits to her grandparents' house. They'd brought her up from the age of six after her parents were killed in a car crash. Sometimes she'd be able to chat with the residents at the old people's home where she spent weekday afternoons cleaning. She tried talking to the members of staff, but they never had much time for her, always having to get on with their jobs.

Vicky wandered down Cobble Street at eleven forty-five just as Thomas parked his Land Rover nearby. They met at the turn-off to Appleby Avenue.

'I meant to catch you earlier but a phone call led me elsewhere. I need your rent.'

'Is it that time already?' They walked down the path, not quite side by side, owing to the lane's narrowness. 'I won't have any money left – oh! I've just been given another part-time job.' They reached Vicky's path. 'Hopefully – oh wow!'

One of Vicky's new next-door neighbours had just let their cat out.

'Look, Thomas! What a lovely cat!'

The fluffy ginger and white feline jumped up onto the four-foot high fence dividing Numbers 5 and 6. With a meow he welcomed Vicky's attentions, mirroring her staring green eyes.

'Why don't you stroke him too, Thomas?'

'Nah. I'm more interested in stroking money. Is it ready, then?'

Vicky kissed the cat's head before leading Thomas indoors.

'Thank you kindly,' he said moments later, counting Vicky's rent. 'By the way, do you still work afternoons at that old codgers' 'ome?'

A few explanations were required before Vicky understood this question. With the translation complete she confirmed that she cleaned there between one and five o'clock. Vicky stepped outside when Thomas left, hoping to see the fluffy cat again, but he'd slinked off.

As Thomas exited Appleby Avenue he almost collided with the large, bearded stranger wearing overalls, a peaked cap, and sunglasses, who'd been watching him talk with Emma that morning.

'Sorry, fellah,' said Thomas.

The stranger nodded in response and, after taking an extended look down the lane, wandered over to a rusty Ford Cortina, climbed inside, and followed Thomas from a distance.


Emma felt relieved when the noon lunch-break arrived. She usually had a salad meal in a pub near Twaddle's factory whenever it was as sunny as today. She enjoyed sitting in the warm fresh air and could walk there in five minutes. Today she almost didn't go, as Thomas sometimes called in. The pub faced Badby's Estate Agents. She eventually decided to chance it, hoping he wouldn't show. The thought of sitting in her car to eat appealed even less than bumping into Thomas, knowing how humid her BMW would be after being heated up from the sun's rays.

Outside the pub, at a table for two, Emma hooked her suit jacket over the back of a chair. Moments later she thanked the waitress for bringing her meal so quickly.

Suddenly the man she wanted to avoid appeared, plonking his pint of lager down beside her glass of mineral water. Emma's smile was as forced as Thomas's was smug. She didn't smile at all when he twice patted her knee as he sat next to her. His eyes flickered between her ample bosom rising in vexation within her satin blouse, and her spectacular legs, one crossed over the other, encased in nylon.

'Have you decided about coming out for some beers with me tonight?'

'I'll have to give it a miss. And I'd appreciate it if you didn't touch my knee.'

'Fair enough. Do you fancy going out tomorrow night instead?'

'Thanks, but no. Tomorrow for me equals work in the morning, relaxing in the afternoon, going out with my sister in the evening.'

Emma's eyes never left her salad while she talked between small mouthfuls.

Thomas's eyes never ceased to ogle the immaculate brunette beside him.

Neither of them noticed the bearded stranger who stepped outside right behind Thomas, carrying half a pint of carrot juice, and sat diagonally facing them. They had no idea that a pair of eyes hidden behind sunglasses now focused upon them. Those same eyes could see under the table and caught sight of Thomas patting Emma's knee as though he was her boyfriend.

Meanwhile, Thomas continued trying to persuade Emma to join him for a night out.

'What if I buy drinks for you *and* your sister?'

'This isn't about me wanting a free night out; it's about me catching up with Hayley. Besides, you'd get bored with two women talking all night.'

'I'll take ma chances.'

'No, you won't.' Emma dropped her cutlery before patting around her mouth with a napkin. 'I want a night out *just* with Hayley.'

She stood up, sliding her arms into her suit jacket.

'Where you going? The bogs?'

'Finesse isn't your greatest strength, is it?'

'Eh?'

Thomas sat stewing while Emma visited the ladies' room.

Whenever she couldn't brush her teeth after eating she chewed gum. Thinking this looked common, she always sat somewhere out of sight to chew for five minutes. Once Emma was satisfied that her perfect teeth were clean, she topped up her lipstick, hoping Thomas wouldn't be waiting outside for her.

She decided to leave via the front way, but something resembling an OAPs' outing had begun filtering through the door like a tortoise race. Not wanting to risk being late to work twice in one day, she headed for the back door.

Thomas downed the remainder of his pint as Emma stepped outside.

'I'll walk round the corner with you.'

He banged his shin against the table in his haste to join her. As Thomas followed Emma, the bearded stranger rose and followed him. However, the stranger didn't see what happened between the pub and the adjacent building wall.

Thomas grabbed Emma above the elbow, saying, 'Why are you being so difficult?'

'Get your hands off me!'

She yanked her arm free.

'Listen, I'm expecting a windfall soon and am gonna move to Spain. Why don't you come with me?'

'I'd rather move to the Sahara Desert and live in a tent with a lizard than go anywhere with you.'

She moved away. He followed close at her side.

The bearded stranger exited the beer garden, spotting Thomas grab Emma's arm again as the pair disappeared round the corner. The stranger did not see Emma shake Thomas off, slap his face, and call him an ill-mannered creep. The stranger reached the footpath, unaware that Thomas had a stomach full of wounded pride as he jogged across the road to the estate agents. Nor did the stranger gather that as Emma marched back to work she cursed Thomas under her breath, calling him an uncouth cretin, amongst other things.

\*

Emma remained in a foul mood for the first half of the afternoon. To think she'd even *considered* going out with Thomas! Eventually the thoughts of tomorrow being the last Saturday morning she'd have to work, coupled with the upcoming night out with her sister, eradicated her frustrations.

At three o'clock Emma had her final fifteen-minute break. Whilst sat eating another Stayslim bar her eyes fell on the carrier Bella left on the desk. Emma leant forward, grasping the bag, suspecting Vicky of bringing her something useless or irritating. Instead she found a carton of raspberries inside and a whirl of guilt in her stomach. She remembered last week when Vicky asked her if she liked raspberries. Emma confirmed she did. Vicky eats them every day and sometimes her grandma gives her two big cartons, which she can't always eat before the sell-by date.

Emma thought Vicky was kind for giving her the fruit but she still shouldn't have brought them to the office. She groaned, covering her face. The thought of bringing her to work next week popped back into her mind like a forgotten nightmare.


Vicky stood dusting a window ledge at the old people's home when Lucy – one of the youngest carers – asked why she hadn't gone home yet.

After checking her watch, Vicky said, 'It's only six minutes past four.'

'You're supposed to finish an hour earlier on Fridays.'

'Oh dear! I'm such a twonkle! I was so busy thinking about the fluffy cat that lives next door to me that I'd forgotten today was Friday.'

'Well it *is* Friday. Hurry up and pack your cleaning

things away. Nobody'll pay you extra.'

'Did I tell you about the fluffy cat, Lucy?'

'Yes, just now.'

Lucy began walking away.

'He's really lovely and –'

'I'm sure he is.'

Lucy disappeared round the corner.

Vicky took her time packing her cleaning equipment away, as usual, hoping someone passing by might stop to talk. She didn't see anyone till after she'd finished and was walking towards the front door.

She met Mr Ducklebridge, a senior member of staff, aged about fifty.

'Going home, Vicky?'

'Yes, I – oh! You'll never guess what!'

Mr Ducklebridge halted, stepping from side to side, avoiding eye contact, appearing as though he needed the toilet in a hurry.

'I've no time for guessing games. Just tell me.'

'I've got another part-time job!'

Mr Ducklebridge ceased fidgeting. His gaze met Vicky's unblinking eyes.

'You need to give a week's notice if you're leaving.'

'I'm not leaving. My new job only lasts from nine till half past.'

'Good. That doesn't mess things up for us.' He began sauntering away. 'I didn't want the hassle of advertising for a new cleaner without notice.'

'I'm really looking forward to it because –'

'As long as it doesn't affect your performance here that's all that matters.'

He was halfway down the corridor when Vicky called after him: 'Have a lovely weekend, Mr Ducklebridge.'

'I will do.'


On her way home Vicky stopped to observe a sparrow

perched on someone's fence down Cobble Street. She didn't notice the bearded stranger leaving Appleby Avenue, nor did she see the stranger climb into a rusty Ford Cortina, further down the road, when the sparrow flew away.

Arriving home, Vicky headed to the kitchen to prepare some food. She often talked to herself when alone. Today was no exception.

'Right, let's have – what was that?'

Something banged upstairs. She listened ... Silence.

'I must be hearing things. Right, I'll get some raspberries out, obviously, but what else shall – another bang! I wasn't hearing things!'

Vicky scurried out of her kitchen, through to the living room. She stood motionless on her large rug. Another bang made her jump. She rubbed her hands, glancing at her rug, which featured a picture of a white tiger, teeth bared.

'I wish I could make you come alive and go see what that noise is – as long as you promised not to eat me, of course.'

She gazed around the room, wondering whether to go upstairs. As her eyes wandered they fell on the DVD she was renting.

'I knew there was something else I wanted to ask Emma! Oh well. I've got it for a week. Maybe she'll come watch it with me and have – another bang!'

Vicky ran back into the kitchen. She grabbed her frying pan, knocking over half a dozen other pots and pans, making an almighty clatter.

'Hang on!' she said, after replacing everything she'd disturbed. 'I left my bedroom window open. Maybe that fluffy cat's climbed through it!'

Vicky wandered through to the bottom of the stairs, frying pan in hand.

'Fluffy cat? Are you up there? I'm coming upstairs. If it is you, don't be scared. If you're not the fluffy cat you'd better go back out through my window because I've got a frying pan.'

Vicky ascended the stairs. Her heart was racing when she reached the landing. She kept whispering under breath, 'Please be the fluffy cat! Please be the fluffy cat!'

Both bedroom doors were shut. She checked the spare room ... Empty. Now for hers.

'I'm coming in!'

She grasped the door handle, turned it, gave it a shove and shot backwards, leaning against the bannister. Nobody – male or feline – charged out of her room. Vicky waited until she'd plucked up enough courage to go inside.

The window was open though everything looked normal. She checked her drawers and cupboards. Nothing had been disturbed.

'What a relief!' She put the frying pan on her dressing table, pulled the chair out from beneath it, and sat down. 'I'm glad there're no robbers but disappointed the fluffy cat isn't here.' She rose. 'Better have – another bang!'

Vicky stepped onto the landing. The noise sounded like it came from the loft. She gazed at the hatch. The cover was in place. Everything looked normal.

'Maybe the sound came from next door? I must've been noisy moving in here.'

Vicky returned to the kitchen and continued preparing her meal. At times she thought she heard a noise, though not as loud as before, and guessed this was her neighbours. She didn't need to go upstairs again until bedtime.

Vicky spent the evening home alone as always. Having enjoyed her *Fox and the Hound* DVD so much yesterday she decided to watch it again. The film put her in a good mood. If a fox could become best friends with a hound there was hope for her befriending Emma. She headed upstairs for bed at ten o'clock with a smile on her face.

Vicky stood under the loft for a while to be certain

the noises weren't in her house. As all had been quiet during the last few hours, surely there was nothing to worry about. She decided to go to bed when something above her creaked.

'That definitely wasn't next door!'

Another creak.

'Oh no! I think it's a ghost!'

She shot into her bedroom, slamming the door behind her. If it was a ghost the police couldn't help. She knew from watching television she needed a priest to get rid of it. Although Vicky didn't know any priests, she could go to the nearest church tomorrow and find one, but what must be done *now*? Her grandparents would be in bed. She couldn't phone them for advice. Emma would be angry if she called round at this time. Only one solution was available: get into bed and hide under the covers till morning.

Despite her worries, Vicky soon dropped to sleep. No more noises disturbed her, making her think the ghost didn't know she was hidden under the bedclothes. But later on something interrupted her dream about feeding raspberries to the fluffy cat. She peeped from under the covers at her luminous digital clock: 12:33 a.m. She ducked beneath the bedclothes again. Whatever disturbed her came from the loft. A series of creaks, squeaks, and scrapes followed.

Vicky kept whispering, 'Please be a good ghost and don't get me!'

She thought it was heading downstairs. Several minutes later the noises ceased. She stopped whispering to herself and tried thinking about pleasant things, like seahorses and baby polar bears, which sent her to sleep again.


Vicky got up at seven thirty on Saturday. She stood beneath her loft for a few minutes before going downstairs for breakfast. She figured ghosts wouldn't come out during the day. With the loft being dark it could stay there until nightfall. This allowed time to sort things out.

Vicky changed into her usual 'going out' attire, namely a brown floral-patterned dress with the hemline floating an inch or two above a pair of blue trainers. Following a light breakfast she set off on today's important mission. First stop: a church.

She set off down Appleby Avenue but halted outside Number 1's fence when Emma's door opened.

'Can't talk, Vicky, or I'll be late again.'

Emma opened and closed her gate before stepping into the lane.

'I was just going –'

'Damn! Get from under my feet, will you! You nearly made me ladder my tights!'

When Emma pushed by Vicky, a twig from a tree in her front garden protruded through the wooden fence, brushing against her thigh.

'Sorry, I didn't mean –'

'Thank goodness they're not torn. I would've had to change and been late to the office two days running.'

Emma marched off down the lane, stopping near the end when Vicky asked if she liked the raspberries.

'I tried some last night. They tasted very good. Thank you.'

Emma hastened on. She was about to climb into her car when Vicky spoke again.

'Did Shaun Splatworthy tell you I'll be cleaning the toilets at Twoddle's next week?'

'Yes. It's "Shane Splatterworth" and "Twaddle's." '

'Would you mind –'

'Yes, I'll give you a lift. We'll discuss this later.'


Vicky walked to the nearest church. After tracking down the vicar she asked him to 'exercise' the ghost in her loft.

He remarked that this was beyond his means, suggesting she try a medium, though he believed calling pest control was the wisest solution.

As Vicky didn't know what a medium was, she looked up 'pest control' in the phone book after returning home. She rang Mr Rackendacker, the Rat Attacker, explaining the situation.

Mr Rackendacker said, 'I think you have a problem with bats, not rats. I'm busy today but call me on Monday if there're any more noises and I'll check anyway.'

Vicky would rather have bats than rats. She couldn't afford to take time off work if a rat made her ill with the plague.

She rang her granddad for advice.

'Sounds like squatters've broken in and settled in your loft.'

'No one can get into my house without me knowing, even if they were squatting, and they couldn't get up there without a ladder.'

'Must just be the wind, then, love. Don't worry about it. I'll put your grandma on.'

''Ellow? What's this about a ghost?'

Vicky explained everything again.

'Sounds like you've got bloody woodworm. Those little buggers'll make the place creak. Either that or, like your granddad said, it's just the wind. Can't you ask that neighbour friend of yours to look? If not, phone the council on Monday.'


Shane complimented Emma again for wearing a pink skirt suit and – more importantly – praised her high standard of work. Mr Twaddle also phoned, promising her a bonus for time spent acting as manager. She stepped outside Twaddle's factory after working her last Saturday shift and drove home smiling.

Emma parked her car down Cobble Street, hoping

the good-looking Slovakian neighbour might pop his head outside when she walked down Appleby Avenue, but no. Instead she found the only other neighbour she knew waiting near her fence.

Opening her gate, Emma said, 'I'm going to have something to eat now.'

'I've already eaten, but thanks for asking. Maybe later we —'

'That wasn't an invitation.'

Emma opened her door. Turning round on the step, guilt and impatience mixed together within her, noticing Vicky staring downwards, playing with her hands.

'If this is about work next week, be ready at twenty to nine.'

Vicky perked up.

'I could come round at half eight if you —'

'No! I need my space in the morning. If you're under my feet I'll probably end up forgetting something important. Be outside my gate at exactly eight forty. If you're not there I'll go without you. Goodbye, Vicky.'

'Bye – oh wait!'

'Now what?'

Emma stood in the open doorway, dainty hands on rounded hips.

'Could you come to my house? It won't take long.'

'What won't take long?' said Emma, releasing her ponytail, running her fingers through her dark-brown tresses, resisting the urge to tug the hairs from their roots.

'Would you mind listening to my loft?'

'For goodness' sake! I haven't got time for this nonsense! I'm hungry and want some relaxation before going out tonight.'

Vicky's stare was intense when she said, 'I think there's something up there.'

'Like what? Rats? A wasps' nest? Why don't you phone the council on Monday?'

'I daren't wait that long. I'm worried it might be a

ghost.'

'There's no such thing, you stupid girl!'

Emma felt a pang of guilt, noticing tears well in Vicky's eyes. In a calmer tone she asked if her grandparents or a friend could call round.

'My grandparents don't like stairs and I haven't got any friends apart from you.'

Emma's countenance softened.

'Vicky, there's no such – that's my house phone – got to go.'

Emma's sister Hayley was ringing. During their chat Emma mentioned Vicky's visit.

Hayley said, 'I feel sorry for her.'

'Same here, to a point, but she drives me insane with her stupidity.'

'She's a lonely girl needing reassurance. It wouldn't hurt you to put her mind at rest by going round.'

'Hmph! If I go over there I'll never get away.'

'Don't be silly, Emma. Just check her loft, say there's nothing to be afraid of, and then leave.'

'I'll think about it.'

'Don't be mean, Emma! Go now! You can tell me what happens tonight.'

The chat with Hayley weighed on Emma's conscience, making her postpone lunch. She draped a handbag over one shoulder before opening the front door.

The sight of her tall, blonde, handsome neighbour standing opposite in his garden talking on his mobile prompted Emma to retreat inside. She applied some gloss to her shapely lips, undid her suit jacket, opened the top button of her blouse, smoothed her skirt, took a deep breath, and stepped outside.

Emma's neighbour was still on his mobile with his back to her as she locked the door. A slow walk was in order. The sound of her heels would turn his head. She threw in the odd scrape for good measure, but she reached Vicky's door without receiving the expected result. Only when she knocked did her neighbour finish his call and shout hello. Emma looked in the opposite direction before turning towards him, dimpling-up with the type of smile that could melt the heart of a stone gargoyle.

'Didn't see you there,' she said, while he strolled over, just as the door opened.

'Emma!' said Vicky, stepping outside. 'What a lovely surprise!'

'Ah!' said the handsome neighbour. 'You are busy. I will speak to you another time.'

'Yes, we'll probably bump into each other again.'

Vicky invited Emma inside. They headed upstairs and stood beneath the loft.

'How often have you heard these noises?'

'Yesterday afternoon and last night. I think it's a ghost because it's been quiet all day. Ghosts only come out at night.'

Emma shook her head, sighing.

'Don't be absurd. Besides, you said there were noises yesterday daytime.'

'Yes, but that was in the loft where it's dark. It came out and went downstairs –'

'Was anything missing this morning?'

'No.'

'Then you haven't had burglars. Are you sure it wasn't coming from next door?'

'I thought so at first, but when I stood underneath my loft for about six minutes, something creaked. When it went downstairs I hid under my covers until daylight.'

'You probably dreamt that part. Perhaps what you heard from above was something falling. Maybe a box hadn't been stacked properly and tipped over.'

'I haven't put anything up there.'

'The people living here before you may have left something that's suddenly given way. Depending on what it is, there could be items still slipping out of a tipped-over box, rolling around, causing these sounds to occur at different times. Why don't you fetch your stepladder to check while I'm here?'

'I haven't got a stepladder.'

Emma removed her glasses and rubbed her eyes.

'Well neither do I so – hang on! Maybe there's someone we could ask.'

---

Emma knocked on Number 8. When the door swung open she shot her favourite neighbour another enchanting smile.

He charmed Emma in return with his smile, saying, 'Did you have a good talk with your friend?'

'My friend? Oh, you mean Vicky. She's not – I'm Emma, by the way.' They shook hands. 'As we keep bumping into each other since you moved here two weeks ago – or however long it's been – we should introduce ourselves.'

'Bolek,' he said, releasing her hand.

'Fine!' She turned away. 'Sorry to bother –'

'Wait!' he held up both hands, laughing. 'I get this always with the English.'

Emma folded her arms while he explained his *name* was Bo-*lek*, not Bol-*lock*. Emma interlocked her fingers, staring at the floor, apologising.

'Would you like to come in?'

'No, I only – yes, okay.'

She followed him into the living room. They sat opposite each other in the matching blue arm chairs. Bolek's eyes were drawn to Emma's toned legs as she crossed them, while she appreciated the bicep bulging from his T-shirt as he rubbed his neck. Their eyes met with a tinge of embarrassment, both thinking they'd been caught admiring the other.

'Bol – can I call you Bolly?'

'If you want.'

'I feel – don't take this the wrong way – but I feel like

I'm swearing at you if I call you – you're not offended, are you?'

'No, is okay.'

After several minutes of chat, Emma mentioned not eating lunch yet.

'I also have not eaten. Maybe we –'

A knock on the door interrupted them. Emma remained seated as Bolek went to answer it. He returned with Vicky.

'There you are!' She held her palm to her chest. 'I was getting worried.'

'I'm fine.' Emma stood up, blushing. 'I was about to ask Bolly if he had a stepladder we could borrow.'

He did and they could.

Minutes later, after Emma explained to Bolek why they wanted to check the loft – without mentioning Vicky's ghost theory – the women made their way back to Number 5. As Emma was about to go indoors, Bolek swaggered down the lane, asking her to wait. She passed the ladder to Vicky, who carried it upstairs.

Bolek was on the verge of asking Emma out on a date when a familiar voice turned his head and Emma's stomach. Thomas approached. He returned Emma's black look with a smug grin.

'I've come for Bollock's rent.'


Emma placed the stepladder beneath the loft, offering to hold it for Vicky, who subsequently announced her fear of heights.

'Well I'm not climbing up in three-inch heels!'

'Can't you take them off?'

'Good idea. I'd love to stand on ridged metal steps in my stocking feet.'

'Stockings? I thought they were tights?'

'They are – I didn't mean – oh for crying out loud! Do you have some trainers I can borrow?'

'Yes, but they're not black.'

'It doesn't matter what colour they are! I'm not worried about complementing my clothes while I'm in a dingy loft.'

When the trainers proved to be a size too small, Emma settled for a pair of wellington boots, after assuring Vicky it made no difference to her that they had pictures of butterflies on them. She sat on the chair in Vicky's bedroom, swapping footwear, muttering under her breath how she was right in what she'd told Hayley about not getting away.

As Emma slid on the last boot, Vicky said, 'I've just remembered! I've rented a DVD and wondered if you wanted to watch it?'

Walking onto the landing, Emma ponytailed her hair, eyeing up the stepladder, not relishing the thought of climbing it.

'What DVD is it?'

'*The Fox and the Hound.*'

Emma placed a foot on the first step.

'Isn't that a cartoon?'

'Yes, but it's still a proper film.'

'Hold the bottom tight. Not mine, you stupid girl!'

Emma gripped the sides of the ladder and began ascending at a snail's pace.

'Do you want to watch the DVD, then?'

'I might have time tomorrow.'

'When would you come round if you do get time?'

'Come round? I thought – ooh, I thought that shook then!' Emma froze halfway up. 'You are gripping tight, aren't you?'

'Yes. So don't you want to watch the DVD?'

Emma continued her sloth-like climb.

'I thought you were letting me borrow it because you'd already seen it.'

'I've watched it twice but it's so lovely I thought it'd be nice to see it again with a friend.'

'I'll decide tomorrow.'

She reached the hatch and pushed off the cover.

'If there're any spiders up here I'm not going in.'

'Did you see Nigel outside?'

'Nigel? Hmph! If you mean that mouse-sized spider on that web between your bins, yes, I did see it. Why don't you get rid of it?'

'Ooh no! I like spiders.'

'Well I don't!'

Emma took her mobile phone from her jacket pocket. She used the glow from the screen to search for a light switch. Once located, she flicked it on and climbed onto the top step.

'There're boxes scattered – what's that?'

'Please say it's not a ghost.'

'Of course it's not, you stupid girl!'

'Thanks.'

Emma pulled herself into the loft. She slinked across the wooden panelled floor, towards the far wall, keeping an eye out for arachnids. The object she'd spied peeping out from behind a beam was a locked metal briefcase. She inspected it before returning to the hatch and lowering it down.

'Ooh, I wonder what's inside!' said Vicky, grasping the case.

'Whatever it is, Badby's can deal with it. It strikes me as suspicious.' Emma held her breath as she placed her feet back on the top step. During her descent she added: 'One or two boxes were on their sides. They probably weren't stacked right in the first place and tipped over yesterday.'

Although this didn't match with the amount of noises Vicky claimed to have heard, Emma put that down to an over-active imagination. She sighed with relief when setting foot on the landing. She brushed off specs of dust from her thighs, skirt, and jacket.

'Do you know who lived here before you?'

'No, they'd already gone.'

Emma sat on the chair, near Vicky's dressing table, swapping the wellingtons for her high heels.

'How long have you lived here?'

'Six months, three weeks, and two days.'

'Hmph! And how many hours?'

'Ooh! Probably seven. Maybe eight.'

Emma folded the ladder and carried it downstairs. Vicky followed with the case. They stood together near the front door.

'I'll return this to Bolly. Bring the case. Thomas might still be there. If not I'll take it to Badby's. They can be responsible for it seeing as this is one of their properties.'

'It's no good, I must have a wee.'

'Can't you hang on? I'm not carrying the steps *and* the briefcase.'

'I've needed a wee for the last seven minutes.'

'I'm not waiting about. I'll leave the Yale latch off and come back for the case if you haven't – if you're not ready.'

Emma walked a tightrope line to Number 8, propping the ladder against the wall. On her return to Number 5 she didn't notice a large figure appear down Appleby Avenue.

The bearded stranger – still wearing overalls, sunglasses, and a peaked cap – sauntered down the lane. The hidden eyes observed Emma's graceful form enter Vicky's house, reappearing seconds later with the briefcase.

When Bolek answered Emma's knock, she said, 'Thanks for lending me the steps. I've taken this case from the loft and need to give it to Thomas. Is he still with you?'

The stranger leaned on Emma's fence, pretending to text someone whilst chomping on a raw carrot, listening to the conversation opposite.

'Thomas went back to the estate agents.'

'Well he must have this. I'll drive to Badby's.'

'You still have not eaten?'

'Not yet.'

'If you like, you could –'

'Damn! I've – sorry – I've forgotten my handbag.'

Emma returned to Number 5 and strolled into the living room. Should she announce her departure? No. Vicky would try keeping her there. Emma needed lunch and a relaxing afternoon before going out with Hayley.

She was about to go when the *Fox and the Hound* DVD near the television caught her eye, pricking her conscience, almost making her go tell Vicky she was leaving, but the thought of another annoying conversation wiped out any guilt. Instead she headed for the front door with her handbag and the briefcase.

She opened up, almost colliding with the bearded stranger at the other side.

'Good grief!' said Emma, pressing a hand to her bosom.

In a squeaky voice, the stranger said, 'I'm Ivan. I do odd jobs for Badby's. I'll take that case to Thomas.'

'Have you any ID?'

'Is that a mouse be'ind you?'

'What!' Emma spun round. 'Where –'

'Don't move!' Ivan stepped inside, closed the door, and pressed the large end of a carrot against Emma's back. 'Don't turn round or I'll blow an 'ole in you! Go through to the living room!'

She edged forward, hands raised.

'Open the door!'

Ivan nudged her back with the carrot. Emma turned the handle. They entered the living room.

'If you shoot me the neighbours will hear and –'

'Drop the case! Toss your bag aside!'

Emma complied.

'There's money in that, isn't there?'

'Like you don't know – face forward!' Ivan twice prodded her back with the carrot. 'Kneel down. Put your 'ands be'ind your back.'

Emma's instinct was to spin round and kick Ivan in the shins, but thinking a gun was pointing at her she cooperated with gritted teeth.

Once Emma was kneeling upright, with wrists crossed at her lower back, Ivan put the carrot on the floor and plucked a roll of inch-wide insulation tape from an overall pocket.

'I've put ma gun down but can soon reach it if you try ought daft.'

'For goodness' *sake*!' said Emma, grimacing as the tape began winding round her wrists.

She'd considered stating that this wasn't her home, though reconsidered, suspecting Ivan may decide to wait for Vicky. Emma figured if she complied, Ivan would take the briefcase and go. She assumed Vicky was still in the bathroom or upstairs and would free her once she returned.

Suddenly Emma felt Ivan's carrot-breath on her neck whilst fingers fumbled near her bosom. She'd left her jacket and top button of her blouse undone. Were the remainder about to be popped open?

'What the hell are you doing!'

'Don't flatter yourself.'

Rather than ripping Emma's blouse open, Ivan pinioned her arms to her body by coiling numerous layers of tape above and below her breasts, without brushing a hand against them, despite their immensity and continual vexed heaving.

Once her arms were secured, Ivan manhandled her face down on the carpet.

'You pig! The further you take this – Ouch!' Unwelcome hands grabbed Emma's calves. 'Don't touch me, you creep!'

'Calm down! I'm no fan of bossy busty brunettes in binoculars.'

'I pity whomever you are a fan of – Ouch!'

Emma cursed as her slender shins were brought to

rest on a pair of thick thighs and her ankles were taped together.

''Ow long 'ave you and Thomas been together?'

'We're *not* together! He's almost as vile a pig as you are!' The vile pig turned Emma onto her back and seized her calves. 'Get your dirty hands off me!'

Ivan forced her to lay with heels stabbing the floor and knees pointing to the ceiling.

'You're not with 'im? Yeah, yeah, and I'm blinking balloon.'

'A stinking baboon, more like – Ow!'

Ivan tied Emma's legs up, above and below her knees, ignoring her protestations.

'I bet Thomas is getting ready to do a runner. No doubt you were going with 'im.'

'You complete idiot! Thomas is not, has not been, and never will be my boyfriend.'

'I've seen you with each other loads of times.' Ivan pocketed the tape and pulled out a large handkerchief and a long strip of cloth. 'Thomas came to see you off to work one morning and you were at that pub together. I saw 'im touching your thigh under the table.'

'And I had a go at him for it!'

'Lovers' tiff, eh?'

While Ivan tied a knot in the centre of the cloth and folded the big handkerchief into a square, Emma explained how she'd fobbed Thomas off as they left the pub.

'I was outside today when you told your neighbour about taking Thomas ma money.'

'Only because I'd found it in the loft –'

'So you just 'appen to go where ma cash was 'idden when Thomas knows I'm out on parole. What a coincidence!'

'The reason I went – no!'

Emma turned her reddened face to the floor, compressing her lips, when Ivan aimed the handkerchief at her mouth.

'Don't worry, it's clean. Stop being awkward or I'll fetch that massive spider near your bins and – heh, heh! Thought that'd get your attention!'

'You'll pay for this, you disgusting – Ugh!'

Emma screwed her eyes up as Ivan stuffed the handkerchief into her mouth, followed by jamming the knotted centre of the cloth between her teeth, forcing her lips apart, aiding the handkerchief in flattening her tongue.

'I've 'ad enough of smart-mouthed tarts like you talking down to me during the last few years.' Ivan flicked Emma's ponytail out of the way and laced her gag against the back of her neck. 'This feels like getting me own back on 'em as well as making Thomas suffer.'

Making *Thomas* suffer! Emma responded with a series of offended grunts.

'Last night I decided to teach 'im a lesson by snatching you today.'

'Mmmmph!'

'That's easy for you to say, heh, heh! Let's get you upstairs in case anyone comes knocking at your door.'

Ivan opened the living room door before scooping Emma up off the carpet and carrying her from the room.

As they began ascending the staircase, Emma kicked her bound feet against the bannister, hoping the noise would alert the next-door neighbours that something was wrong. However, another threat of tucking a mammoth spider down her cleavage made Emma relax – despite being anything but relaxed – in Ivan's strong arms.

So far she'd been too angry to feel scared and now believed Ivan never intended to shoot her. She regretted not putting up a fight, yet at first she couldn't know how far Ivan would go, making it chancy to resist capture with a gun prodding her back.

During the past few minutes Emma deducted she was dealing with a thief, not a killer. A thief out on parole would surely not be as dangerous as an escaped murderer. After all, wouldn't a potential killer threaten to shoot her, or at least knock her out, not intimidate her with an arachnid?

Emma mumbled in fury as she was carried into Vicky's bedroom. Ivan planted her on the dressing table chair and taped her bound ankles to a chair leg.

'I need to move your Beamer in case your bloke comes sniffing round. Once that's done I'll be back for ma car and you. Heh, heh! Thought you'd like that.' Ivan patted her thigh, chuckling. 'Ma cousin shouldn't 'ave crossed me. Nabbing you will make 'im sorry!'

'Mmmmph!'

'Glad you agree, heh, heh!'

After closing the window and curtains, Ivan disappeared downstairs.

Emma forgot her fear of the spider. Her rage returned in earnest, making her face so hot that her skin prickled along her hairline. The instant the front door closed she struggled against her bonds. Several minutes later, with sweat beading on her forehead, finding breathing only through her nose an ordeal, she gave up with a moan.

Surely, she thought, nobody could get away with daylight abduction, especially when it meant Ivan carrying her to a car via Appleby Avenue, onto Cobble Street. Ivan must be intending to kidnap her at night, unless it was all just a bluff.

Emma craned her neck, scanning the room for something to sever her bonds, but there wasn't a sharp object in sight. Besides, with the amount of tape binding her arms and legs and with her ankles tied to the chair, she'd probably end up tipping over if she tried manoeuvring towards the dressing table, the little chest of drawers beside the bed, or the wardrobe in the far corner.

One question kept recurring in Emma's mind: where was Vicky? Had she been kidnapped too? Surely that wasn't possible, unless Ivan had a partner. The likely scenario was that Vicky had left via the back door of her own accord. All properties down Appleby Avenue had a rear yard with an alley behind it leading onto Cobble Street. Yet it seemed odd – even for Vicky – to have wandered off after being so pleased to receive a visitor. After speaking to Bolly about taking the briefcase to Thomas, Emma assumed that when she returned to Number 5 Vicky would be waiting like an obedient child.

She moaned, grasping the irony: Vicky – who always appeared whenever Emma least wanted to see her – was now nowhere to be seen, yet here sat Emma, tied to Vicky's chair! For the first time ever she was desperate to see this girl who'd become like an extra shadow, annoying her with irritating attempts to make friends.

How had that stupid girl talked her into coming over to check if there was a ghost in the loft? If it hadn't been for Vicky, Emma would've finished her lunch long ago and now be taking it easy at home. Her temper exploded. She tried getting free again. Her gag and the layers of tape constricting her like an anaconda ensured she experienced the same futile attempt as before.

Calming down, she remembered Hayley convincing her to check the loft by laying on a guilt trip. Emma cursed Hayley for pushing her into it and cursed herself for listening. Yet that was the point. *She* made the final decision. Hayley didn't put a gun to her back, forcing her into Vicky's home. Emma had been the one who asked Bolly for his stepladder. If she hadn't visited him they wouldn't have had access to the loft. The money would still be undiscovered. Ivan wouldn't have seen her with the case and she'd be at home now. Okay, Ivan intended to kidnap her anyway, thinking she was Thomas's girlfriend, but the chances of this happening would've been unlikely if she'd been home, rather than outside with a case full of money.

The only good thing to come out of Emma's predicament was meeting Bolly properly. At least he'd be there when this was over. In the meantime, how long must she endure this frustrating ordeal?

Thirty minutes passed. Emma heard a key turn in the front door. Hopefully this would be Vicky. Heavy footsteps on the stairs suggested otherwise. The bedroom door opened.

'Sorry to keep you waiting,' said Ivan, munching on a carrot.

Emma groaned, staring daggers. Her stomach rumbled with hunger and unease as she watched Ivan unravel the tape securing her to the chair. She moaned in fury as once again those hated arms gathered her up.

Ivan carried Emma downstairs and dumped her on Vicky's large rug. She thrashed around like an electrified fish, realising her captor's intentions. Ivan soon terminated her struggles and rolled her over three times inside the rug, further muffling Emma's gagged protests; protests that escalated when she felt herself lifted in the air and humped over a broad shoulder as if she was nothing more than a bath towel. Her discomfort increased several times when Ivan jolted her around whilst opening and closing the doors upon leaving the house.

Outside Ivan began humming 'Little Miss Muffet', drowning out the continual stifled mutterings emanating from the rug.

Emma's temper soared as she was jerked around again when Ivan paused to undo and fasten the gate. Thinking she heard her favourite neighbour's voice, she bleated as loud as her gag permitted, yet a brusque lift and drop on that uncomfortable shoulder left her winded.

Emma had indeed heard Bolek. He'd stepped outside to drop some rubbish into his bin, exchanging greetings with the singing stranger who nodded in response.

No one else noticed Ivan plodding down Appleby Avenue onto Cobble Street. Saturday afternoons were quiet in this little corner of Hull. If by chance anyone happened to look out of their window, just as someone wearing overalls dumped a large rug along the back seat of a Cortina, they'd never assume a woman was wrapped up inside it. Nothing serious like kidnapping ever happens round here.


So where had Vicky been all this time? Well, following her visit to the bathroom she walked through the kitchen, intent on seeing Emma before she went home, but something caught her eye as she passed the kitchen window. A certain feline was prowling along her back wall.

'There's that fluffy cat again! I must stroke him!'

Vicky stepped into the back yard where she either sat or knelt down with her friend, oblivious of what was happening inside, not glancing at her watch until after Ivan had kidnapped Emma.

'I didn't know it was that time! Oh! Emma might be sat waiting for me. Goodbye, fluffy cat!'

Vicky kissed her friend's head before returning indoors.

She wandered into the living room. Confusion swept over her like a tidal wave. How had her chair moved? Where was her big rug? Why was there a carrot on the floor?

'That must be Emma's lipstick!'

Ivan had taken Emma's handbag but the lipstick rolled out of it when she'd first tossed it aside.

Vicky sprinted upstairs, shouting Emma's name. More surprises greeted her when she entered her bedroom. Why were the window and curtains closed? How had the chair moved? What was all this black tape doing on the floor?

'Oh no! Ghosts *must* come out during daylight. I think it's taken Emma and my rug!'

Vicky sped across the landing, slid down the bannister, and raced over to Number 1. When nobody answered her knock she scurried over to Number 8 and rang the doorbell.

Bolek greeted Vicky with a smile.

'Hello – I can't remember your name.'

'Bolek.'

'Sorry. I'll call you Emma's friend. Emma's friend –'

'My *name* is Bo-*lek*.'

'How awful! Okay, I'll call you Jasper.'

'No, my –'

'Jasper, I'm worried about Emma. I think she's been taken.'

Bolek's relaxed countenance changed to the type of expression normally caused by constipation. He asked Vicky to explain.

'I found her lipstick near my couch, my rug's gone, my chair's moved, the window and curtains are closed, and there's a carrot on the floor.'

'I do not understand.'

'I think there's a ghost in my house.'

'A ghost?'

'A ghost is something that's sort of dead –'

'I know what is a ghost, but do not believe one has taken Emma. She went to Badby's.'

'I'll see if her car's on the road.'

They both checked. With no sign of the BMW, Bolek's mind was eased, though Vicky still felt concerned.

'Why would she leave her lipstick?' said Vicky, walking down Appleby Avenue.

'Ah!' Bolek nodded. 'Emma say she leave her bag at your house. I think maybe her lipstick fall from it. With her being in the big hurry, maybe she does not realise.'

They stopped near Bolek's gate.

'But why was there a carrot on the floor?'

'Have you dropped it after shopping?'

'Ooh no. I hate carrots – Urgh!'

'So it must be Emma's carrot.'

'It could've been, but what about my rug?'

'Is it expensive?'

'No, but it has a lovely picture of a white tiger on it.'

Bolek raised his hand.

'Wait!'

'Okay, Jasper.'

'I saw earlier a big man with a beard walk by my house carrying a carpet. You have nothing else stolen?'

Vicky shook her head.

'What I think is this: you leave the Yale lock off and Emma forgot to close it when she leave. Soon after she go, the man knock. Maybe he see Emma leave and think she is rich or something, so he try moving the door handle after she has gone. When he realise it is not locked, he walk in and see your carpet, thinking it is expensive. When he move it, he drop his carrot, and closes the lock without knowing. Why not phone Emma if you are still worried?'

'I don't know her number.'

'Try Badby's. Speak to Thomas.'

Vicky went home thinking how lovely 'Jasper' was, hoping they'd become friends. She was usually shy around men, especially good-looking ones under thirty like her neighbour, but he'd made her feel comfortable. One day she hoped to have a boyfriend. So far no men had shown any interest in her. Jasper had been kind, but she could tell he wanted Emma for his girlfriend. That was okay though, providing he made her happy.

Vicky phoned the estate agents. The answering machine came on. Of course! They close at one o'clock on Saturdays. She rang Thomas's mobile, leaving a voicemail, asking whether Emma delivered the briefcase. Five minutes later he phoned back, saying he'd never seen Emma, but what was this about a briefcase? Vicky related finding it in the loft and the mystery of her living room and bedroom. When she'd spoken to Bolek she'd forgotten to mention the insulation tape lying on the bedroom floor but remembered to tell Thomas.

He sounded serious when assuring Vicky not to worry about Emma. He knew nothing about a case or a stranger and hung up before she could ask anything else.

\*

Vicky spent half an hour watching television, unable to concentrate, even though she liked documentaries about penguins. She phoned her grandparents, arranging to visit them.

Vicky took the longer scenic route through Hobbleforth Park. From here she went down Hyde Road, which featured a pub undergoing refurbishments, although there was nobody working this weekend. Two vehicles resided in The Lions' Den car park.

'That looks like Emma's LBW!'

Vicky scurried over. She couldn't remember Emma's registration number, but recognised the *Wow!* sticker in the back window.

'Woe and behold! It *is* Emma's car! Why has she come to a saloon with cardboard stuck to all the windows? Ooh, there's a squirrel!'

Vicky crept towards the nearby hedge and knelt down, gazing at the squirrel a few feet away. She looked away from it when the sound of footsteps caught her ear. Her view was obscured by the cars. She rose just as a large person wearing overalls dropped a set of keys and stooped over to retrieve them. Vicky felt a twinge of fear in her stomach, prompting her to hide inside a gap in the hedge. She watched Ivan walk past the other car – a Ford Cortina – and climb into the BMW. After taking a crunch from a small carrot, Ivan drove away.

'Jasper said he saw a big bearded man carrying a carpet! I think he's kidnapped Emma and stolen her car and my rug ... I'll check the saloon.'

The back door had been forced open. Vicky entered the pub and headed to the bar area. She found Emma's empty handbag in a corner on the floor and popped it inside her carrier. Vicky didn't own a handbag. A carrier sufficed just as well. She tiptoed forwards, stopping when a muffled sound caught her ear. She followed the intermittent mumblings to one end of the pub where she found several tables with chairs piled on top of them spread out in front of a long seat against the wall. Two tables in the corner were placed end-to-end, pushed close to the long seat, on which Vicky discerned her rug.

The stifled noises grew more consistent as she moved the chairs and pulled one of the tables away from the seat. Slight movements were evident at the quiet end of the rug. Vicky peered down the mumbling end, spying the top of someone's dark-brown hair.

'Emma!'

The noises paused before recommencing in earnest.

Vicky hugged the top end of the rug, easing Emma off the seat. The bottom end slid off, whacking the floor. She lay the upper end down and rolled it all the way across the large barroom. Nothing unravelled. She stood at the other side and began pushing it back the way she came. Three more turns and Emma – red-faced and dizzy – rolled out of her stifling confinement.

Vicky helped her sit upright, leaning one shoulder against the wall, before unlacing her gag.

'Pah!' Emma spat the handkerchief from her mouth, screwing her face up in disgust. 'Urgh! I've never been so outraged in my entire life! Do you have any water in that carrier?'

Luckily Vicky could oblige. She held a bottle of water to Emma's lips, quenching her thirst.

'Thank goodness for that. I don't think the thug who kidnapped me will be back any time soon, but just in case he surprises us, you'd better untie my legs first so we – what's the matter?'

'I'm worried about laddering your tights.'

'For goodness' sake! I'm not getting ready to –' Emma sighed. 'Sorry. Don't worry. For once it doesn't matter. Just untie me, please.'

While Vicky began searching for tape-ends with her

short fingernails, Emma recalled her abduction, the things her captor had said, spoke about Thomas, and about the money.

'To think that brainless baboon Ivan kidnapped me to punish Thomas!'

'Why?'

'The idiot thinks I'm his girlfriend!'

'Why?'

'Because – Vicky, I've just thought! How did you find me here?'

Emma listened, surprised by how lucky she was to be discovered by chance.

About ten minutes later, with the tape all removed, Emma thanked Vicky, who helped her up on two numb feet. They sat together on the nearby long seat, opposite the far one where Emma had resided in a much less comfortable position. She clenched her fists and rotated her feet, fighting off her pins and needles. A few minutes later she took a chapstick from her jacket pocket and smoothed it over her lips.

'At least your lipstick hasn't rubbed off.'

'Yes, that was my main concern the whole time while – what time is it, by the way?'

'Twenty-seven minutes past three in the afternoon.'

'Half three! It was about one when that wretched pig barged into your house and ruined my day!'

'This is all my fault for asking you to look in my loft!'

'It's not your fault. I blame Thomas and Ivan. Don't cry! You're letting them win.'

'But what if you'd got a snuff ball up your nose? You would've surrogated!'

'You mean "fluff ball" and "suffocated", you stu – I mean – listen! I wouldn't have suffocated. I haven't been inside that rug the whole time.'

Vicky sniffed, wiping her eyes.

'Really?'

'Really. Being gagged made it hard to breathe, but –

don't keep crying! Ivan would laugh if he knew. I was going to add that I have good sinuses and –'

'Sinuses? What's one of those?'

'Never mind! Anyway, the drive here didn't take long. Once that thug carried me in here he taped me to a chair. He only wrapped me inside that damn rug again before he left in case anyone came nosing round. I spent a long time listening to him boasting how clever he was in fooling Thomas by snatching the cash and making *him* suffer by kidnapping me! He heard me tell Bolly that –'

'Who's Bolly?'

'Our Slovakian neighbour.'

'Oh, I call him Jasper.'

'Jasper?'

'Well, when I asked –'

'Never mind that now! As I was saying, that brainless thug heard me tell *Bolly* I was taking the briefcase to Badby's. He said Thomas hid the money in your loft for him before you moved in.'

'Are they robbers?'

'Ivan's on parole. He kept bragging how he'd skipped his last check-in or whatever it's called. He contacted Thomas – who claimed to be away this weekend – about collecting the money. Suspicious, Ivan stole a car and drove to Hull yesterday. He's been following us ever since.'

'So he absconded you because he thought you stole his money.'

'Absconded? "Abducted"! He'll pay for this. And damn him for taking my bag!'

'Ooh!'

Vicky plucked Emma's handbag from the carrier.

'Typical! Nothing's left inside. I kept my credit cards, phone, and all sorts in here. It's a shame you don't have a mobile. We could've called the police by now.'

'There's no point me having one. Apart from work and Badby's I only know my grandparents' number … Did I tell you Ivor drove off in your car?'

'No, but – it's "Ivan" – no, but I knew that was his plan. He went to get the briefcase keys from Thomas and took my car to ensure he'd believe I'd been kidnapped. When Ivan left just before you found me, he promised to let me out when he returned, but only to carry me down to the cellar! When he arrives in Spain tomorrow he intends phoning Thomas to inform him of his "girlfriend's" whereabouts! *Tomorrow*!'

Vicky placed her palms together, as if to pray, touching her nose with her index fingers.

'What if he'd forgotten to phone Thomas? You would have died of salvation if nobody found you!'

' "Starvation"! No I wouldn't. Ivan the Intolerable pointed out that if Thomas didn't come tomorrow I'd only have to wait till the builders arrived for work on *Monday*!'

'You must've been so scared!'

'Scared! I was too furious to be scared! Ivan is nothing more than an overgrown school bully; an opportunistic thief who only managed to kidnap me through sheer luck. Damn him for tricking me with that "There's a mouse behind you" bluff!'

Vicky didn't understand but nodded anyway.

Emma, welcoming the return of her circulation, mentioned how hungry she felt.

'Oh! Did you leave a carrot on my living room floor?'

'A carrot? Don't be so –' She sighed. 'Sorry. No, I tend not to leave vegetables on living room floors.'

After a minute's silence Emma put a hand on Vicky's arm and said, 'I want you to know I'll be eternally grateful to you for helping me today.'

Vicky didn't know what 'eternally' meant, but understood that for once Emma was pleased with her, not annoyed. She smiled, feeling proud of herself.

'If you want me to do you any favours, just ask. Forget what I said about not waiting for you before starting work at Twaddle's. If you're not at my gate on time in the mornings I'll knock on your door. Maybe I could buy you something special to thank you for rescuing me. Is there anything you'd like?'

A sweet smile crossed Vicky's face. This is what having a friend felt like.

'Will you watch my *Fox and the Hound* DVD with me?'

'That's the least I can do. Does tomorrow afternoon sound good?'

'That would be lovely, but won't you be recovering from what's happened today? Don't people get shocked or something when criminals do awful things to them?'

'Hmph! Some may suffer from shock but I'm not going to become all weak and reclusive because of that great ape Ivan or that smug creep Thomas! I still intend going out with my sister tonight.'

Her empty stomach grumbled.

'Sorry, Emma.'

'What for?'

'I think I just pumped.'

'No, it was – never mind!' She rose, adjusting her skirt, blouse, and jacket. 'My circulation's getting better. We'll leave after I've visited the ladies'. Let's put everything back how it was. If that thug gets back and thinks I'm tied up, he might potter around before unravelling your rug, giving us chance to get away and call the police. They'll arrest him before he can make tracks.'

As Emma headed to the ladies', Vicky loosely rolled her rug up, laid it along the seat, and began replacing the furniture. She dropped two chairs, drowning out the sound of the back door opening. She was too preoccupied to sense Ivan creep up on her.

'Don't move!'

Vicky squawked and ran. She'd almost made it to the back door when Ivan grabbed her arm and flung her to the ground. With another scream she was back on her feet, avoiding a pair of swooping arms. She ran in circles round the big central bar.

Hearing the commotion from the ladies', Emma

hastened to the barroom with a metal toilet roll holder in each hand, grasping them as one might clutch a knife to stab downwards. Her shoes made no noise on the thick carpet as she slinked towards Ivan, who'd caught Vicky at last. They both knelt upright where the chase began. From Emma's perspective it appeared as though Ivan held a gun to the sobbing Vicky's back.

She froze as Ivan told Vicky: 'I'm putting ma gun down but can soon reach it if you try ought daft.'

Emma's mouth gaped open: the gun was a carrot! Suddenly Vicky's story about the vegetable on the living room floor made sense. She also remembered Ivan chomping on one during her captivity. She'd been kidnapped under the threat of a carrot. Enraged, she slinked forwards. Her ambush was foiled at the last minute when a spider of epic proportions hurtled across the floor, skimming over the pointed toe of her shoe.

Ivan rose as Emma shrieked.

Vicky scrambled to her feet.

Emma's fear vanished with the spider. She attacked Ivan with the toilet roll holders.

Ivan deflected her blows, saying, 'I couldn't find Thomas; 'ad to prise case open; it – argh! – it was full of paper. You was gonna fleece – ow! – fleece your boyfriend!'

'He's *not* my boyfriend, you idiot!

Emma knocked Ivan's sunglasses off, revealing one blue eye, one green.

'Hit him with a chair!' shouted Emma, as a strong hand seized her left wrist.

Ivan spun round upon hearing a clattering noise. Vicky had tugged at two interlocked chairs so hard that she fell over backwards with the furniture.

The distraction gave Emma chance to break free. Down to one toilet roll holder, she tugged Ivan's beard with her empty hand. To her surprise she tore it off, leaving just the moustache. She ducked a flailing arm and grabbed at Ivan's groin, finding nothing but overalls.

Vicky untangled the two chairs whilst on her knees. She tried swinging one at Ivan whilst rising to her feet, but stood on the hem of her long dress and fell flat on her face.

Emma's shock realisation that Ivan was a woman threw her off guard, costing her the second toilet roll holder, though thanks to Vicky causing more background clatter, Ivan-the-woman looked round again, allowing Emma to stab a three-inch heel into his — or rather *her* — foot.

*She* hopped backwards, tripped over a toppled chair, banged *her* head on the floor, and knocked *her*self out. The hat — featuring a black wig sown into the back and sides — fell off, revealing short blonde hair underneath.

'Sorry, Emma,' said Vicky, back on her feet, sobbing. 'You were so brave! I was just a useless twonkle!'

Emma, catching her breath, assured Vicky that she'd already proven her worth today.

'Let's search this ogress's pockets before — what's wrong?'

Vicky stood gaping at Ivan's face.

'So is Ivor really a woman?'

'Yes!' Emma knelt down, yanking off the false moustache. 'Hah! There's another one underneath! Let's see if we can find out who Ivor — Ivan! — really is.'

Emma drew many items from the overalls, including carrots, insulation tape, her keys and credit cards, other keys, money, and a fake ID featuring the name 'Ivan Newman'. She undid the overalls to search Ivan's jeans' pockets. She discovered a *real* passport, belonging to Ivy Spivey. She found her mobile in another pocket but couldn't get any reception.

'Right, Vicky! Grab an arm and — not mine, for goodness' sake! This big lump's! We're going to take *Ivy* to the cellar and leave her for the police to collect.'

Moving the big woman proved a difficult task,

especially for little Vicky, but they managed to drag her behind the bar, leaving her on the top few cellar steps. Emma slammed the cover shut as Ivy started regaining consciousness. They made haste in placing chairs on top of the cover.

'Let me out, you bloody bitches, or else –'

'Or else what? I said you'd pay for what you did to me. Don't worry, though. You won't be down there for long. Some friendly policemen will soon be here to take you to a room with a barred view.'

Ivy swore, pounding the cellar cover. The weight of the chairs prevented her from budging it.

'Will the police let me have my rug back?' said Vicky, as Emma led her from the pub, into the car park.

'I'm sure they will, though you'll have to leave it for now.'

'I ought to sell it really and buy a smaller one in case Ivor escapes from prison and tries absconding you again.'

As they approached the BMW, Emma phoned the police, who were grateful for the call. Ivy had skipped parole and would now have to serve the remaining half of her six-year sentence. Emma shot Vicky a satisfied smile, saying Ivy would get put away for even longer after today's events.

'She'll regret – I don't believe this!' Emma, hands on hips, stared at the car number plate. 'That carrot-crunching troll's changed my registration plate!'

'And your *Wow!* sticker's gone.'

They jumped into the car.

'Well, he – *she* – did plan on stealing my car, so I guess things could've been worse.'

'I'm just glad you're okay.'

'Thanks to you, I am.'


Minutes later they were walking down Appleby Avenue. Emma invited Vicky round to her house with the police wanting to speak to them both. Vicky wanted to phone her grandparents from home first to explain – in brief – why she hadn't visited them as planned.

Emma strolled into her kitchen to drink a glass of water and eat some raspberries. Her long overdue lunch would have to wait till after the police interview. She entered the living room. She'd forgotten how comfortable it was to sit on an armchair. Emma was poised to phone Hayley when a noise distracted her. Did someone knock? Perhaps Vicky gave the door a light tap, feeling nervous about talking to the police.

Emma stepped towards the living room door, freezing when it opened from the other side. Her mouth dropped.

Thomas appeared, holding a black briefcase.

'How on earth did you get in here?'

'Badby's spare keys.' Thomas observed the fading red marks beneath Emma's tights and near the corners of her mouth. 'Didn't expect to see you. Thought ma cousin 'ad swept you under the carpet. 'Ow did you escape?'

Emma glared at him with fiery eyes, not intending to reveal what really happened and put him on guard.

'Some snooping children found me gagged and tied to a chair in a derelict building after your gorgon cousin left me for Spain.'

Thomas rested his case on the sofa and clicked it open. Not only was it full of Ivy's money, it contained 'extra' rent money he'd collected … and a gun.

'Throw your mobile on that chair.'

Emma's eyes darted between Thomas and the weapon he brandished. This was no carrot. She tossed her phone aside, advising Thomas to hand himself in before making things worse. She'd guessed during her captivity that he'd been the cause of the noises in Vicky's loft.

"And myself in for what? The cash I've fleeced off ma cousin isn't stolen. Ivy made it through years of forgery. Only thing I've done is fiddle Badby's accounts.

Besides, I've arranged a boat ride out of 'ere. I need to get going. Unlock that and get in.' He alluded to the cupboard under the stairs. 'I'll take any light valuables of yours then leave.'

Emma folded her arms, crossing one calf in front of her opposite shin.

'How did you get into Vicky's loft last night? I assume that's when you swapped the money in the case for paper?'

Thomas nodded. As Emma predicted, a smug smile crossed his face as he bragged how he'd brought a ladder, knowing Vicky didn't own one, and entered the loft.

'Goggle-eyes told me she finished work at five. The dizzy cow came 'ome about forty minutes early.'

When he'd heard Vicky downstairs, he pulled the ladder into the loft, staying put till he thought she'd be asleep, thus avoiding confrontation. Thomas figured if she heard him sneak out during the night she'd be too scared to investigate what was happening.

'I'm off abroad earlier than planned. Now move!'

Emma's blazing eyes never left Thomas as she edged towards the cupboard.

'I'll leave front door unlocked for when your sister comes.'

'How considerate of you!'

Emma glanced at the clock. Vicky would soon arrive, followed by the police. She stopped in front of the cupboard, asking why the money was originally hidden in the loft.

Thomas smirked, explaining that six months ago someone grassed Ivy up for forging documents. The law didn't know about her £20,000 savings. Ivy asked Thomas to hide the money in case she got arrested.

'5 Appleby Ave 'ad been vacant for months cos of the damp patches in the bedrooms and the shitty kitchen cupboards. Badby's manager told me to organise the repairs. I kept fobbing 'im off, saying the workmen 'ad problems with materials. I used the place for card games. I stashed the case in the loft, thinking nobody'd ever be dense enough to rent such a crappy-looking property. Vicky moved in a week later. Now get in the cupboard!'

Emma placed her index finger on the bolt.

'Why wait so long to take the money?'

'I wanted to fiddle more cash out of Badby's foreign tenants and Vicky. Then you moved 'ere, making me 'ope you'd join me abroad when I'd built up ma savings. You could've been rich, living in a villa from tomorrow.'

Emma drew back the bolt.

'I'd rather live under my stairs than in a palace if it meant living with you.'

'In that case shut up and get in!'

Emma opened the door, ducked down, and grabbed her long winter coat.

Thomas trod forward as she stepped back out. She spun round, throwing the coat over his head. She kicked her pointed shoe against his shin – twice. Hopping, he dropped the gun. After dragging the coat from his head, his nose met Emma's fist, his groin felt her knee.


Vicky wandered towards Emma's house when the fluffy cat trotted down the lane, meowing at her. She crouched down to stroke him as Bolek returned home from the shops. Vicky told 'Jasper' about 'Ivor' 'absconding' Emma.

Vicky, accompanied by Bolek, was about to knock on Number 1 when the door flew open. Emma appeared, holding Thomas's gun. She passed it to Bolek. He noted that the weapon was an expensive type of water pistol.

After a quick explanation the trio headed to the living room. Emma and Bolek stood side by side. Vicky hovered a few paces behind.

Thomas had recovered from Emma's attack well enough to reveal one last trick in his pocket. He held up an unopened flick knife, warning everyone to get back. They *jumped* back, for when he flicked the knife open, the blade shot away from the handle. The bemused Thomas was too slow to defend the knock-out punch to his forehead, courtesy of Bolek.

Thomas woke up as the police arrived. He couldn't be charged for the possession of the money he'd taken from the loft, as it couldn't be traced, but following Emma's statement regarding Ivy kidnapping her, she related Thomas's boasts about gambling at Vicky's house before she moved in, about him fiddling Badby's accounts, and about him entering her house uninvited, threatening her with a water pistol, promising to steal her valuables.


Once their statements had been made, Bolek invited Emma to his house for a meal, treating her to the best food she had tasted in a long time.

'Would you like to go out with me tonight?' he said, after they'd eaten.

'I'd love to, but can't. I'm having a girls-only evening. I'm free tomorrow night though.'

Later on Emma kissed Bolek goodbye before walking outside with a smile decorating her beautiful face. She looked forward to spending more time with Bolly in future.

She knocked on Number 5. Vicky appeared, smiling, waving hello. Would she like to come out with Emma and Hayley tonight? A sweet smile crossed Vicky's face. Nobody had ever invited her out before.

'I'll be ready in sixteen minutes!'

'We're not going for two hours yet. Come round later. We deserve some fun after today's nightmare. Let's show the likes of Thomas and Ivy that they can't keep us down. I've been thinking as well. On Monday I'll phone Badby's and insist they fix your house up.'

'Thanks, but nothing's broken.'

'I know that! I mean the damp and such like. I'll tell the manager to sort it out quickly or I'll threaten to do an interview for the local paper, detailing how poor your living conditions are. Thomas'll get named and shamed anyway. Badby's won't want more damning publicity.'

'Thanks for being so kind, but you know, I don't want to sound ungrateful –'

'What's the matter?'

'Although I'd love my house fixing I'd rather it stayed the same and you watched my DVD with me instead.'

'You stupid girl! I'll still watch it with you! Bring it to my house tomorrow. Hayley would like to see it too.'

Vicky arrived at her friend's house that evening. She followed Emma into the living room, carrying a sports bag.

'This is your half.' Vicky placed the bag between them on the couch. 'We've got ten each.'

'What?' Emma pinched the bag's zip.

'Didn't I tell you before?'

'Tell me what?'

'I'm such a twonkle! The police said Ivor's money can't be trailered, or something. Because it was in my loft I'm allowed to keep it, but I want to share it with my best friend.'

Emma unzipped the bag, discovering £10,000 in wads of cash, leaving her dumbstruck. She appeared so serious that Vicky thought she'd offended her.

'I can give you more if you want. You were much braver –'

'You stupid girl! Of course I don't want more!' Emma embraced Vicky. 'What did I do to deserve a friend like you?'

# ABOUT THE AUTHOR

Phil Syphe was born in 1975 and grew up in the East Yorkshire village of North Newbald. In 2012 he graduated from the University of Hull with a degree in Creative Writing & English. He lives in Hull where he works from home as a copy-editor & proofreader and writes novels.

www.philsyphe.snappages.com

www.grammareyes.weebly.com

Printed in Great Britain
by Amazon.co.uk, Ltd.,
Marston Gate.